THE COMEBACK SERIES BOOK TWO

MARCIE SHUMWAY

Cover Design: MGBookCovers; www.melissagilldesigns.com

Photographer: Eric Battershell Photography; www.ericbattershell.com

Model: Ryan Lee Harmon

Editor: All About the Edits; aboutabouttheedits.wixsite.com/editingproofingbeta

Interior Formatting and Design: T.E. Black Designs; www.teblackdesigns.com

JULIE

THE MORNING AFTER A WEDDING could go any number of ways —from a hook-up gone horribly wrong to the hangover from hell. As I stretched, naked, under the cotton sheets covering me, the verdict was still out. My head had only a dull throb and my stomach didn't seem ready to revolt. I'd consider that a success.

The sunlight peeked through the window and caressed my eyelids. Not yet ready to face the day, I was about to roll over when a muscled arm swung over my side and a very solid, defined chest pressed against my back. Suddenly, it all came rushing back.

I had stuck to just a couple of drinks at the reception because I'd wanted to keep my wits about me. My entire life had been about doing the "right" things, and the men in my friend Avery Hall's life made you want to do all the wrong ones. Every single one of them was gorgeous, tattooed, and incredibly sweet. I did not do one-night stands, as a general rule, and I had slept with a total of two men in my life—well, now three. It hadn't been my intent to change that because of a musician, bar owner, or a construction worker.

Obviously, my lady parts had made the decision for me, just as they wanted to again, one more time before I had to leave. I pushed my ass back into his pelvis and was rewarded with a moan and a twitch of his already hard member between my butt cheeks. An internal battle raged. I never did things like this. Should I enjoy this man one more time or did I bail out now?

His large hand cupped my boob through the fabric of the sheet and my hips bucked back against him of their own free will. *Guess I know my answer.* While he kneaded and pinched, I stretched and purred, keeping my eyes closed against the outside world. For just a little bit longer, I wanted to pretend it was just us.

"You're playing with fire, boss lady." His breath was a soft timbre in my ear that sent shivers down my spine.

Before I could respond, I was on my back with a lean body between my legs, and I was looking up into his handsome face. His hair, longer on top, flopping onto his forehead. My hands were somehow locked in his above our heads and his cock pulsed against my already throbbing clit. The smile on his lips was faint, but it was there, as it always seemed to be. Locking my legs behind his back, I ground against him, watching as his blue eyes darkened with lust.

"Maybe you should take care of it then," I teased.

"Careful what you wish for," he replied, his voice low.

I closed my eyes again and soaked in the feeling of his lips on my body. Open mouthed kisses teased my neck and traveled across my collarbone. When his warm breath whispered over my nipples, I moaned, squeezing my legs together.

"Evan," I breathed on a sigh.

"Julie," he responded in a growl.

I was pulled from our bubble by a sound from outside the

room. My eyes popped back open and I froze. Evan continued his ministrations, however all the warm fuzzies were gone for me. A toilet flushed upstairs, then quiet murmurs in the hallway and a cough from downstairs all reminded me we weren't alone.

"Stop," I told him as I unlocked my legs and tugged on my hands.

He didn't question my request; just simply rolled off me and onto his side as I pulled back the sheets and got up. I grabbed his dress shirt from the floor and slipped it on to cover myself before turning to look at him. Evan had his head propped up on his hand and made no effort to hide himself as the sheet rode low on his hips, his cock straining against his lower belly.

"You're a huge help," I muttered, diverting my eyes before I decided to climb back in his bed.

"I'm not going to hide the fact that I want you," he replied, a smile in his tone. "That much was obvious before you asked me to stop."

"Everyone is getting up!" I hissed, surprised to find my bag near the door.

"You don't think they didn't hear us, or Avery and Cooper last night?" he asked, the sound of him throwing back the covers and pulling on boxer briefs filling the room.

I stopped in my search for my underwear and turned to look at him. Had we really been that loud? Avery and Cooper were a given, they were newlyweds. How was I going to face them all? This was Evan's fault. Him and that tattooed arm, those stunning blue eyes, and that package currently being cradled lovingly in black cotton. His smile grew as I took him in, yet my eyes narrowed.

"I'm sorry," he quickly apologized, his hands going up in surrender, flashing those sinful dimples. "I'll even go see if the coast is clear for you to make it to the bathroom."

My eyes narrowed further when he opened his bedroom door and stepped part way out. He was still clad in his boxer briefs that fit him like a second skin, and the idea of others seeing a piece of what I had didn't sit well with me. Wait? What? This had been a one-night thing. Why should I care if any other women checked him out?

"You're good," he let me know, coming back in and heading to his closet.

"Thanks," I mumbled, grabbing my bag in one hand and clutching the too-large shirt in my other as I moved past him.

When I was settled in the bathroom with the door closed behind me, I dropped my bag and let out a long breath. It was time to put on my business face and not make the walk of shame I was already going to have to do any worse than it was. I looked in the mirror and let out a moan. My long brown hair was sticking up all over the place from the hair spray we had plastered in it the day before. My makeup was smudged, though my brown eyes gleamed, and I looked like I had been thoroughly sexed.

"Shit." I quickly locked the door and started the water in the tub for a quick shower.

By the time I was cleaned up and in a pair of dark skinny jeans with a dark blue V-neck long-sleeved shirt, I was feeling a little more human. Once my eyeliner, mascara, blush, and a touch of lip gloss was applied, I began to feel like the powerhouse I knew I was. I ran a comb through my locks and after a few scrunches with my fingers, I let it be. It could dry on its own today. My last look in the mirror was much better than the first one.

Picking up my bag, I unlocked the door and made my way back to Evan's room. The door stood open and I stepped in to find him gone. I put his shirt on his bed and hesitantly looked around. It fit him. His sleigh bed sat in the middle—he had even made it before going downstairs—with two nightstands on either side. The lights on each were simple as was the rest of the décor. A small Smart TV was on a bureau across the room, and it sat at an angle that he could see from either the bed or the recliner tucked in the corner by the window. The dark colors on his bed and on the walls above the headboard were masculine and surprised me, given his light-hearted nature.

As I turned to head back out, I caught a whiff of something that could only be described as his; the combination of some AXE body spray and Irish Spring soap. My core instantly warmed and I felt my nipples harden. The memory of his hands on my body filled my head, and I had to shake it as I walked to the door. My brown knee-high boots had been brought up and set by the door, so I pulled them on and, with my bag in hand, did one final look around to make sure I had everything.

It was time to face the music. Taking a couple of deep breaths, I rolled my shoulders and pulled them back. Standing up straight, I moved into the hallway. I could do this. I was a strong woman who owned her own company, and no man was going to turn me into a pile of mush. It was just a hook-up. Nothing was going to change.

EVAN

"Fuck." I cringed when I heard the click of the bathroom door behind her.

Shaking my head, I pulled on a pair of well-worn jeans and a navy and hunter green flannel button-up shirt. Rolling the sleeves up on my forearms, I sat down on the edge of the bed. The smell of her vanilla perfume instantly hit my nose and I felt my dick twitch. *Down boy*, I chided; there was no way we were getting any more from that lady today. Stupid early risers ruined any chance I had of getting any this morning. She had been soft and warm against me until the sounds of everyone getting up had her freezing. I knew I had been lucky as it was the night before to have her, but it hadn't meant I wanted it to be over.

After pulling on my socks and boots, I went to my closet and did a quick round with deodorant and body spray to try to cover the smell of sex and alcohol that still clung to me. I turned around and started buttoning my shirt, when I saw Avery putting Julie's boots by the door. She gave me a wink and a knowing smile before quietly turning and going back down stairs. Damn. This wasn't going to be fun.

I made my bed and heard the water turn off, signaling Julie was finished in the shower. Knowing it would just make her more uncomfortable if I was here, I headed to the stairs. While I made my way down, I thought of all the things I could say to the others to keep them from making any comments. Julie wasn't your normal wedding hook-up. The feeling of her in my arms was different than any other women I'd been with. It had felt right. Her sighs and soft mewls the night before had left me shaken to the core. I wasn't a virgin, by any means; hell, the road life of the band didn't allow for much of that. It was lonely and sometimes the alcohol wasn't enough. Yet, she had ruined me for anyone else.

"Well, it's about damn time you grace us with your presence," Cooper Hall joked as I entered the kitchen.

The entire band, Avery, Maggie Andrews, and Lexie Waterhouse were all seated around the kitchen table and at the bar, digging into breakfast. I felt my cheeks warm and I chuckled when his new wife slapped him upside the head. She wasn't going to let him get away with anything. I kept moving and made my way to the coffee pot. That was the first thing my body needed before I had to deal with the shit I knew was coming from all of them.

"You had better not say another word," Avery warned as she got up and gestured for me to sit down between Coop and our lead singer, Chris Hines. "She's not only my friend, but she's my boss too, and I want to keep my job."

I flinched slightly at that reminder. I didn't want to be the cause of any issues between Julie and Avery. Clearly, the wrong head had done all the thinking the night before. I started to open my mouth to apologize to her, but her hand came up and she shook her head before I could. Putting a plate in my empty hand, Avery leaned up to press a kiss to my cheek. I smiled from ear to ear, and laughed when I heard my bandmate mumble something behind me, about touching his woman.

"She touched me first," I reminded him as I sat down.

This time, he hit *me* upside the head, and everyone chuckled. I shrugged him off and kept my smile in place as I filled my plate with scrambled eggs, pancakes, and bacon. These people were my family. Chris had formed our band, Dark Roads, when we were in high school. I played bass, Cooper, the drums, and Matt Waterhouse played steel guitar. Our country music with an edge, along with Chris's uncle, Lee, had us climbing the charts in no time. We had barely had our high school diplomas in hand when he had whisked us off to Nashville. While it had been an amazing almost eleven-year ride so far, we were all tired and looking for a bit of a break, Cooper and myself more so than the other two. Coming home to Maine had been just what we had needed.

It not only allowed us all to recharge, but had also brought Cooper and Avery back together. The two of them had been inseparable our last few years of school, yet the idiot had left her high and dry when we signed our contracts. He had never stopped loving her, though; if anything, he had fought it for ten years.

Now they were married, and I had never seen him happier. I wanted what he had. Hell, I wanted what Maggie and Lexie had. Lexie was Matt's little sister. When she had turned eighteen, she joined us in Tennessee. She had become our little groupie and there, she met her wife, our lawyer. The two hit it off instantly, and the love between them was evident.

"Damn," I heard Matt mutter beside me as his elbow hit mine.

I jerked my head up and saw Julie pausing briefly as she entered the room. Her hair was still wet from her shower, and fell down her back in long waves that had me fighting the urge to tangle my fingers in it. Her wide eyes were slightly weary, however she held herself ramrod straight. This woman was a force to be reckoned with. The V-neck shirt she sported teased a bit of skin, and the jeans clinging to her legs made me want to scoop her up and carry her back to my bed. I brought my elbow back into Matt's stomach a little too hard, and heard him cough slightly.

"Keep your eyes on her face, brother," I hissed, surprising myself.

I wasn't normally a possessive man. This woman brought out a whole other side of me. I relaxed in my chair when I felt Cooper's hand on my shoulder. Julie didn't seem to notice the activity at the table as she moved toward Avery and for that, I was grateful. I didn't want her to feel any more uncomfortable than she had earlier this morning.

"I really should go," I heard her say after she gave her friend a big hug. "I have a lot to do at the office."

"At least eat with us before you do," Ave pleaded.

Julie's gaze shifted to the table, where we were all sitting, quietly. All conversations had gone silent and eating had ceased. Her eyes passed over mine in a fleeting glance, and I knew that she had been going to take the opportunity to bail while everyone was occupied. She was embarrassed about the night before, even though a word hadn't been spoken about it.

"I'm good," she assured her, putting a hand on her arm to stop her from getting another plate. "I'll get something on the road."

Julie was already moving to pick up her bag and turn toward the door. I started to get up to walk out with her when Avery caught my eye and shook her head slightly. My ass hit the chair with a *thud* and my friends steadied me to keep it from going over. I wasn't a complete jerk; I should have been the one going outside with her, not Avery.

"What the hell?" I muttered, as activity around the table resumed.

"The Foster charm was lost on that one, huh?" Matt joked as he shoveled food into his mouth.

"I'm not quite sure," I admitted, running a hand down my face.

"She's a skittish one," Cooper observed, "despite her tough exterior."

"That she is," I agreed, smiling. "Guess I'll just have to work on that."

JULIE

"**W**HAT THE HELL WAS I thinking?" I mumbled to myself as I made the trek back to my apartment.

Unfortunately, two hours gave me plenty of time to replay the reception, the activities after, and my bailout this morning. The whole thing was out of nature for me. I was always so put together, overthinking every step I made. Shaking my head, I merged onto the interstate.

"It was those damn eyes," I answered myself.

And the dimples, and the tattoos, and the muscles... Who was I kidding? It was the whole damn package. He was a member of a well-known edgy country rock band, whose personality was as sweet as his body was hard. Evan was different from any of the guys I had ever dated. Maybe that was why I had thrown caution to the wind.

Now, I was going back to reality. The one place I didn't really want to be. Moving to Maine to help get the new branch of Lane & Son up and running, was sounding better and better. A new start, a clean slate. Change had never been something I handled well, but maybe it was time.

When I pulled into my driveway a little while later, I sighed. My apartment was actually a duplex I owned. I rented the other side to my receptionist, Kelly Boudreaux, and her friend. I had purchased the building on a whim, when living in the city had become too much. It was twenty minutes from the office and had ten acres of land with it. Other than the occasional car, it was a quiet piece of property.

Today, it seemed *too* quiet. As I carried my bags to the door and unlocked it, I noticed the silence. Normally, it was a breath of fresh air from the confines and sounds around the office; however, I was quickly missing Avery and her crew. The ones I thought I had needed to run from.

Not wanting to be alone with my thoughts, I changed my clothes, putting on workout pants and a tight-fitting long-sleeve shirt. I pulled an armband over my shirt and settled my phone in it before lacing up my sneakers. Tuning my Amazon Prime Music to a Top Country station, I popped my earbuds in and stretched.

The minute my feet hit the pavement, I felt all the stress of the morning melt away. My muscles slowly started to warm and with Lauren Alaina pounding in my ears about picking the road less traveled, I picked up the pace. Here, was my little piece of heaven. The wind, the steady *thump* of my heart, and the burning in my legs.

I had despised working out for as long as I could remember. My mother had passed on her generous curves, yet I had gotten my father's metabolism. Sweets had been my weakness as a kid; however, I never gained an ounce. I hated the gym; the leering from the men and the gossip of the women. Running had only recently become my best friend, a means to escape the world.

My life had taken some turns in the past year. Ones that I hadn't seen coming. Physical exertion had become my way to deal with it all. Or hide from it. I guess it all depended on how you looked at it. While my girlfriend and new business partner had been finding love again, I had been losing mine.

My feet churned faster at the thought. Oh, how I had been such a fool. How hadn't I known what was going on right under my nose? As happy as I was for Avery, I secretly worried about her and Cooper. He was a drummer, with a past full of women. How did she trust him not to stray? I had found a prominent businessman with no skeletons—or so I had thought—and that had blown up in my face.

I stopped, bending over to catch my breath. Seconds later, moving again so I didn't cramp, I turned and headed back toward my house. I guess the saying was true; you couldn't judge a book by its cover. Ryan Cobourne had been the perfect man on paper. He came from a well-to-do Boston family, old money, and had earned his MBA from Harvard. Little had I known, he had been hiding a few secrets of his own.

My feet carried me back into my drive on autopilot. Once I got into the house, I stretched and let my mind wander back to my soon-to-be ex-husband. Ryan had been a doting yet hard-working spouse. The long nights didn't worry me since I had them as well; even the weekends weren't a huge surprise. Our marriage had been great those first few months, and I had even been considering talking to him about kids. It was a juggle I had been ready for.

Stripping down, I stepped into the shower. The smell of Evan rolled off me despite my earlier one. There was one thing that him and my ex had in common—women. I had flown out to Las Vegas to surprise Ryan on our anniversary and found him pounding into his supposed secretary when the manager of the hotel had kindly let me into his room. What a surprise it was.

Clearing my head of the memories, I put my face under the hot water. With my eyes closed and the steam swirling around me,

Evan's gorgeous one popped into my head. I didn't want to think about him or the fact that I was probably just another notch in his bedpost. I shook it, trying to dislodge the image, but his blue eyes were burned into my brain. I still remembered the first night I had met him and seen them.

"Come on!" Avery exclaimed, tugging on my hand.

"Honey, we're only going to go as fast as the line," I told her with a laugh, trying to keep pace.

"Oh, don't worry about that." She giggled.

We moved around the line of people waiting to enter the arena. I gave her a questioning look, but she just smiled and tightened her grip. She led me around the side of the building and I pulled her to a stop when all I could see was a large bearded man. He didn't look all that happy, and I wasn't going to be held responsible for anything happening to her.

"Ave," I whispered.

"It's fine, Julie," she assured me. "I promise."

She resumed her track toward the guy. As soon as we got close enough to talk to him, a grin broke out on his face and his features softened. His arms opened as we took the last few steps, and Avery released me to be engulfed in a bear hug.

"Hello, sweetheart," the man greeted, dropping a kiss on her head.

"Hi, Mikey," she returned, squeezing him tightly before leaning back and gesturing to me. "This is Julie."

"Well hello, beautiful," he drawled out with a wink, as he shook my hand then brought it to his lips to plant a kiss on the back of it.

"Enough fraternizing, man," I heard a voice chide with a chuckle. "Coop isn't going to want drool all over his woman."

"This one isn't his," the bearded man stated with a grin as he released my hand with another wink.

"Ain't that the truth," came the reply from the unknown voice.

"Enough, boys," my friend scolded good-naturedly, no bite behind her words.

I turned to see the other guy she was approaching to hug, and my breath caught in my throat. It was obvious that he was part of her fiancé's band. *He wore well-worn jeans with holes at the knees, worn brown cowboy boots, and a dark blue t-shirt that clung to his muscled chest. His baby blue eyes sparkled and seemed to pop out of his face, along with his ear-to-ear smile. My lady parts pulsed when he reached up to adjust his backwards ballcap, causing his biceps to tighten and his tattoos to dance.*

"So, this is the famous Julie?" he questioned as he held his hand out for mine.

"Yes," I let out on a breathy sigh, causing me to cough to try to cover it.

"Nice to finally meet you," he said, his smile growing with my reaction to him. "I'm Evan."

I felt my cheeks instantly warm under his gaze, and when his lips touched my hand like Mikey's had, I jumped. The shock was surprising. Avery had told me all about him, but nothing had prepared me for meeting him in person, or my body's reaction. He was every woman's wet dream.

My eyes snapped to my friend's and I gave her a glare. Avery laughed softly and shrugged her shoulders. Evan's eyebrows raised at our silent conversation, but he didn't seem fazed in the least. Moving between us, he threw his arms over our shoulders and started to lead us down the long hall into the venue.

"Let's go, ladies," he urged. "It's time to have some fun, Dark Roads style."

I'm not sure why I had ever let Avery talk me into going with her that night. Most of it was probably because I hadn't wanted her to go alone, and neither Jen, her best friend, or Abby, her sister-in-law, could go. I wasn't normally into the concert scene, but I had needed to keep busy while Ryan was out of town on a business trip, and going had been the perfect fix. I hadn't taken into consideration that we would hang out with the band so much, since my friend had been newly engaged to the drummer, or that I would have a pair of blue eyes burning holes into me all night.

After lathering myself up with lotion following my shower, I put on leggings, a long sweater, and left my feet bare. I ran a comb through my hair and made my way back to the kitchen. Opening my laptop that was sitting on the island, I turned it on. I took some leftover soup from the prior week and put it in the microwave, then waited for it to heat up. Grabbing a water from the refrigerator, I heard the computer alerting me of new emails. I wasn't surprised, and moved to check them while the soup was still warming.

"That was quick," I commented, as I noticed I had one from Avery's personal email that had been sent mere minutes before with a link in the heading.

Evidently, she had received the link from her wedding photographer and she couldn't wait to share them, so I clicked on it. Everything was quick to load and before I knew it, I was scanning through pictures, ignoring the sound from my microwave, letting me know lunch was ready. There were some beautiful ones of the newlyweds, some wonderful ones of all of us girls in the wedding party, and some great ones of the band. My hand froze on my mouse when I came to one of Evan and myself.

I was so engrossed with it that I brought my face closer to the screen rather than enlarging it. If I was someone from the outside looking in, I would have thought we were a couple. I remembered the moment exactly. I had sat down to take a break from dancing at one of the empty tables and was rubbing one of my sore feet. Evan had come over and plopped himself down in a chair in front of me, flashing me that unforgettable smile, and had pulled my foot into his lap to rub it himself. The photographer had caught us smiling at each other, me leaning in a bit to put my hand on his arm. I had been telling him that he didn't need to do that.

My phone vibrating on my counter caused me to jump, breaking me from my trance. While I reached out blindly to grab it, I clicked my mouse to make the picture larger. Evan's smile was easy, as it always was, yet there was something in the way he was looking at me. I couldn't quite put my finger on it. My smile was grateful and my eyes...wait, that couldn't be right. I had the same weird something in my eye that I couldn't figure out.

I shook my head; I was probably just seeing things. I looked down at my phone and swiped my finger across it to bring my new text to the forefront. It was from an unknown number, but when I read it, I knew immediately who it was from. I guess my running out this morning hadn't given off the vibe I had hoped.

Since you didn't stick around this morning, boss lady, you owe me breakfast 😉

EVAN

"WHAT ARE YOU GRINNING FOR?" Coop questioned, as I set my phone down next to the radio that was blaring some 90's punk rock.

"I'm teasing boss lady," I responded with a smile.

"You're not going to let that go, are you?"

"Let what go?" I asked, putting a twenty-five-pound plate on the squat bar with the others already there.

"This thing with Julie," he stated simply, like he was speaking to a child.

"It's not a *thing*," I told him with a growl, narrowing my eyes.

There it was, that possessive feeling again. I watched as Cooper's eyes widened, and his mouth dropped open in surprise. I'm the good-natured one of the group, with a smile always on my face and an easy going demeanor. Something about that woman left me feeling protective, like I needed to defend her, though I was sure she could do it just fine on her own. I know he didn't mean anything by it; the tone came out before I could stop it. Shaking my head, the grin returned, and I got back to loading the bar.

"You got it bad," he chuckled, going back to his bicep curls.

"I might," I agreed. "She's different. Special."

Rather than dwell on the Julie situation, I got in place in the squat rack and pushed the bar up across my shoulders. I let the routine of my weight lifting take me away from everything else. It was the one time that my head was always clear. I couldn't have been happier when my friend had said he wanted to put one in the small basement of the house that he renovated. We had one at our house in Nashville, and we used it all the time when we weren't in the studio.

I let out an "*Oofff*" as I put the bar back in place once I had done my reps, and stepped back. Rolling my neck and shaking my legs out, I added more weight for my last set. The only sounds in the room were the *clinks* of the weights as we adjusted them, the music from the small radio, and the occasional grunt as we finished our last, heaviest reps. It was comforting in a way, and since it was only the two of us, there was no need for conversation.

Figuring that the newlyweds would want time alone, Chris and Matt had made themselves scarce right after we finished eating breakfast. Lexie and Maggie had been close behind. When I had lingered, unsure where to go, since I really didn't *have* anywhere else to go, Cooper had barked at me to change and meet him downstairs. Avery had kissed my cheek before placing a long lingering one on Cooper's lips, then muttered something about spending time with her father, who had recently beat cancer for a second time.

"So, really, what's up with you and Julie?" Coop asked when he finished his last set and moved to the open space on the floor to stretch.

"When did you become the nosy one?" I responded with a

chuckle. Usually, I was the one who wanted to know everything going on.

"I've been taking lessons from my roommate for the past eleven years," he returned with a grin.

"Aren't you supposed to be spending time with your wife?" I questioned, hoping the change in conversation would deter him.

"Can't, with you always underfoot," he joked.

I felt the jab instantly to my heart, even though I knew he was teasing me. When I was growing up, the Hall house had been my getaway. My father had never been around; hell, my mother didn't even know who he was, based on what little she would tell me. Connecting with Cooper, Matt, and Chris had been what had saved me from the lost boy I had been. I don't think I would have been a troublemaker because that wasn't in my nature, yet I had been lost and lonely.

Once I hit high school, my mother was home less and less. There was always food in the refrigerator, and I had clean clothes, so I wasn't neglected, per se. Yet, I had never felt love until I stepped foot into Cooper's house. His mother recognized the need I had the moment I met her. Marcia hugged me every time I was in the house and jostled and teased me right along with her own boys. I spent more time there once the band got serious, and almost never went home unless I was summoned.

It had been a blessing that just before I graduated, I had turned eighteen. I was a legal adult when I signed my paperwork with the label and Dark Roads, preventing her from having any involvement. Not that she had wanted any in the first place.

"I was kidding, man." Coop turned serious as he put a hand on my shoulder.

I looked up at him from where I sat on the bench and flashed him a smile. I knew he had been, but he was also right. It was time for me to look for some place to live. He and Avery needed their time alone as a couple, and I needed to start settling back in here in Dewart, since it was now going to be our home base.

"I know, but it *is* time for me to find a place, now that we have everything figured out with the label," I replied, wiping my face with my towel. "Maybe I'll call Mrs. Hood and see if she knows of anything in the area."

"Actually, Avery and I have been meaning to talk to you about that." He coughed, seeming to struggle with the words.

"Oh?"

"Since I have a fairly large plot of land, we didn't know if you would want some acreage to put a house on," he said. "Somewhere back near the wood line."

I was speechless. My friend, my brother, had picked out this piece of property for two reasons. One of them being that it was in our hometown, and another because it was large and secluded. When he returned to renovate the home, and had started seeing Avery again, I'd tagged along and told him that I would be right here with him when we weren't on the road. I sure as hell hadn't seen him wanting me this close when I moved out.

"You're not fucking with me, are you?" I asked, trying hard to keep the smile on my face from getting any bigger.

"Would I do that?" he questioned, feigning innocence. "Okay, I would, but not about something like this."

"If you don't mind me being here, I would love to," I told him truthfully.

"Of course I don't mind," he answered, bringing me in for a hug when I reached out to shake his hand. "I'd rather have you share this land with me than my actual brothers."

I laughed at the comment. While he was close to both Willie and Rick, he and I shared a bond like none that I had ever experienced. He was my best friend and as far as I was concerned, my brother. With no siblings of my own, he was the closest thing I had to one. Excitement built inside me as we moved upstairs to clean up, talking the entire time about the piece he thought would be perfect to build my house on, and that he had already reached out to Dale, Avery's father, to see if his company, Grind Construction, could start the groundwork when I was ready.

I grinned uncontrollably as we separated to clean up. We decided that we would walk out this afternoon and take a look, putting stakes in the ground where the house would be and where he would like to split the property. I knew there would be a lot of paperwork to get everything moving, but I didn't care. My dreams of having a real home to call my own were coming true. Grabbing a water out of the refrigerator, I trotted upstairs to my room.

Stepping inside, I stopped dead; the smell of vanilla overtook me and instantly made me hard. Julie's beautiful face came to my mind, and somehow I knew that she needed to be the one to share that home with me. Sure, I hadn't known her long, but when you knew, you knew. Now I would have to figure out how to convince her.

Grabbing clean jeans, a t-shirt, and boxers, I made my way into the bathroom to take a shower. My dick tented my athletic shorts and no matter how much I tried to clear my head, Julie's gorgeous face kept coming back. I think I had known that first night I met her at the concert that I wanted her. When my lips had touched the back of her hand and a spark surprised us both, I had known, despite having another man's ring on her finger. She was it for me.

Setting the water as hot as I could bear it, I stripped down and got under the stream. I braced my arms against the wall and let the water roll down my back to loosen my tight muscles. The smell of vanilla filled the steam of the shower and I closed my eyes, letting my mind wander back to the reception and when I had made my move.

"Why did Avery have to pick all married women for her bridesmaids?" *Matt complained as we stood by the bar in the tent, waiting for our drinks. "Didn't she know we needed some ass after she took one of our bandmates?"*

Chris and I chuckled. It was true; Ave had picked her sister-in-law and best friend to stand beside her, and they were both married. However, her boss Julie was no longer wearing her wedding band. That, I had noticed from the moment she had come down the aisle. She had one on the night of the concert, but it was noticeably absent tonight. Not wanting the other guys to make a move on her, I had kept quiet.

Once I received my drink, I turned and surveyed the room. The woman that was filling my head was sitting down at a table, alone, watching the people dancing, rubbing one bare foot with her hand. A soft smile played on her lips. Giving the guys a nod, I moved toward her, being careful to stay out of her eyeline. When I slid into the seat near her feet, she jumped slightly.

"Evan!" she gasped, placing the hand she had been using on her foot over her heart. "You startled me."

"Sorry, sweetheart," I apologized, pulling her foot into my lap and starting to rub my thumb up the arch. "That wasn't my intent."

Her eyes closed as I applied more pressure, and I heard a soft moan before she covered it with a cough. Her brown orbs popped back open and her cheeks pinked with embarrassment. I continued to rub and smiled at her. She returned it and pulled her foot out of my hands. Before she could move away, I reached down to grab the foot still in a boot, quickly removing it and treating that arch to the same attention I had given the other. Rolling her eyes with a grin, she leaned toward me and put her hand on my arm.

"Thank you, but you really don't need to do that," she whispered, a slight catch to her voice as I dug my thumb into a sensitive spot.

"I want you to see how good I am with my hands," I told her in a low voice, flashing her a smile I knew showed my dimples, and running my tongue over my lips.

Julie's eyes grew dark and hooded with my actions, her mouth opening slightly. When I pulled her foot closer to the heat growing in my lap, next to my hardening cock, her teeth nibbled on her lower lip. Her nails bit into my arm slightly and I leaned closer, bringing my mouth to her ear.

"I seem to have a problem that needs to be taken care of," I said on a growl. "Care to help me with it?"

She nodded slightly when I pressed a light kiss to her temple and I sat back. Just as I was getting ready to release her foot so I could stand, she pushed her toes slightly into my crotch, causing my eyes to cross. Grabbing her before I came like a teenager during his first time, I slid it down my thigh and back to the floor. My eyes met hers and a naughty smile graced her lips. Damn, I was in trouble.

"Well, that didn't help," I groaned, coming out of my daydream.

I was hard as hell, and who knew when I would be seeing her again. It would be sooner rather than later, if I had my way, but I knew it would take some convincing on my part to get her back in bed. The alcohol had lowered her inhibitions that night. She had been responsive and just as into it as me, yet shy, so I had a feeling she hadn't been with a lot of men. With her smell all around me and the help of some body wash, I made quick work of my hard-on. I came with such force, I let out a loud groan, one I was sure Cooper had heard from downstairs.

Once the ache between my legs was at a dull roar, I washed up and finished with my shower. Drying off, I ran a brush through my hair and quickly dressed. I grabbed socks from my bedroom and made my way back down to meet with my friend. I drew up short when I entered the kitchen and found him leaning on the counter with a shit-eating grin on his face.

"Did Julie join you up there?" he asked.

JULIE

I'M PRETTY SURE I JUST liked torturing myself. Yeah, that had to be it. I had no logical reason to go back to Maine, Avery could handle everything herself. I trusted her judgment on new clients. I was just going to see the new office and meet with her about a few things. It wouldn't be all day, then I could head home and go for a run. Just a quick trip.

Traffic was light, so it was fairly uneventful. That wasn't a surprise given that I had left the house at five. I hadn't been able to sleep and after pacing for a half hour, I had grabbed my bags and hit the road. Bags—plural—yep, a work bag and an overnight. I wouldn't need it, but just in case.

When I pulled into the Halls' driveway, I cringed. I was way too early. Avery had texted me and assured me it was fine, since they were all early risers anyway, but I felt extremely guilty. I should have just gone straight to the new office building. They were newlyweds, for God's sake, they should be enjoying the time they had together before the band left to go on tour again. I knew Evan was living there, but still.

Stopping behind Avery's SUV, I turned off my car and sat for a moment. The sun was rising and it promised to be a beautiful spring day. I could do this. I would grab my friend and we could head straight to the office. There was no guarantee I would run into Evan. *I could do this.*

A few deep breaths later, I was stepping from my vehicle and headed to the door. Voices carried as I brought my hand up to knock, and was startled when it whipped open before I could. The man I had been hoping to avoid stared back at me. He was just as surprised as I was, but it was only a second before his killer smile kicked in. Dimples and all. Damn.

My body instantly reacted as he took me in, from my dress slacks to the light jacket I wore over my teal button-up blouse. My nipples perked in my bra and I was instantly grateful I had worn a padded one along with a camisole underneath my dress shirt. At least he wouldn't be able to tell. Letting out a breath, I kept my back straight and tucked my hands in my jacket pockets.

"Evan," I greeted with a slight smile, a professional one that I had schooled myself with for years.

"Boss lady," he returned, the smile amping up in wattage. "Here to take me up on that breakfast?"

"Evan Michael Foster! You let her in this minute," Avery scolded from behind him.

I saw him flinch slightly at the tone in my friend's voice and I had to stifle a giggle. What was it about him that set me back twenty years in my maturity? His smile remained despite her comment, and he swept an arm in front of himself to invite me in. I moved by him, keeping as much distance as I could between us, and found Avery giving Cooper a quick hug and kiss.

"The guys were just leaving," she informed me, letting out a yelp as Cooper gave one last squeeze to her butt before moving away.

"Good morning, Jules," he greeted, tipping his hat.

"Good morning, Cooper," I returned.

Both Cooper and Evan wore baseball caps, hooded sweatshirts, jeans, and work boots. Today, they just looked like normal men, not the members of a famous country band. It always amazed me when I saw them, especially when all four of them were together. The brotherhood, the energy, the sexuality. It all seemed to ooze from their pores.

"We will bring you breakfast before we head out," she told them as she moved to the refrigerator.

"Make sure you eat," her husband told her, getting ready to head out the door Evan still held open. "You're looking a little pale."

"Just what a woman wants to hear," I heard her mumble.

This time, I allowed the smile to grace my face at their antics. They truly were an adorable couple, even if I wasn't so sure about Cooper and his past. Before I could move to help her, my eyes met Evan's. His baby blues sparkled with mischief and the grin on his face was just as concerning. I narrowed my eyes at him and felt my smile slip. The only response I got as I turned was a chuckle from him, as the door clicked shut behind them.

"So, are you ready to fill me in on what is going on between you two and the reason you aren't wearing your wedding ring anymore?" Avery asked as soon as I was fully facing her.

"Nothing and no," I replied simply.

"Okay, first of all, here we are, Avery and Julie, not boss and employee," she reminded me, putting a pan on the stove. "Second of all, I'm not blind, and I know you spent my wedding night with him."

"That was a lapse in judgment," I told her as she mixed eggs and milk together, her color going more green now than just pale.

"I would believe that if I didn't see the way your body reacts to him," she chided as she reached into the refrigerator for some precut veggies. "It's the same way mine does every time Coop walks in a room."

"Okay, fine," I let out, my tone exasperated. "I'm attracted to him. What woman wouldn't be? Have you seen those damn eyes or those dimples?"

"Oh yes, Evan is quite the package," she agreed, turning on the stove to warm the pan. "He would definitely be my second pick of the band if I had to choose."

Her comment left me stunned. It also reminded me that he was basically an icon. Women all over the world knew who he was and dreamed of being with him; heck, some *had* been with him. I was just another conquest. Someone to chase while he was here before he went back on tour. I was better off to forget about him.

"Stop that right now," Avery's voice broke into my thoughts.

"Stop what?" I asked, as she poured the mixture from her dish into the pan.

"Overthinking," she said, covering her mouth with her hand.

"Ave..." I started.

"I'll be right back," was all she got out before dashing from the kitchen toward her bedroom.

Moving to watch what I assumed was an omelet she was making, I turned the heat down a bit and set out making another. I knew even one large one would only be enough for either Cooper or Evan, so another would have to be made. I was just folding the first one over the cheese I had added when she returned, promptly pulling a chair out at the table and plopping down into it. She had a cold cloth and was wiping her face, but at least some pink had come back to her cheeks.

"Do you care to share?" I asked her while I put a couple of pieces of lightly buttered toast in front of her.

"Thank you," she smiled gratefully, nibbling slightly on one before she answered. "I'm pregnant."

"Oh Avery," I cooed, coming to kneel in front of her. "I'm so happy for you. I know you were excited to start a family."

"I am…" she replied, not looking at me.

"Why do I sense a 'but' coming?"

"There is no but," she finally said. "Just a lot of concerns. We are starting the new office, Cooper will be leaving on tour for most of my pregnancy, Dad is just starting to feel better."

"Now who is the one overthinking," I reprimanded, tapping her on the nose and getting to my feet to flip the omelet one last time. "Everything will be fine."

"I know it will, it's just…"

"Stop!" I cut her off. "It will. No buts or anything else. I'll be here to help with the office, and I'll help keep an eye on you for Coop."

"What?!" she exclaimed, getting up to come to stand beside me as I finished with the first omelet and started on the second. "How are you going to do that? That's an awful lot of commuting."

"I was thinking about finding a small place to rent up here. I can help with getting everything running, now that we will actually have the office space set up, and will be here when the guys leave if you need anything."

I think we were both surprised by my comment. She never expected me to say it, and I hadn't planned on doing it until she had told me she was expecting. I would worry about her being here alone while her husband was gone, not to mention the stress she would put on herself as she got everything organized with the business. I knew she was fully capable, but I didn't want her pushing herself if she didn't need to. My Massachusetts office could run itself.

"You're not going to rent a place," she informed me after we worked in silence for a while.

"Oh?" I raised a brow at her.

"You can stay here. In the spare room," she stated.

I turned to look at her sharply, almost causing her to drop the pan of bacon she was removing from oven. She let out a laugh when she saw my face, but I saw her pale again when she caught a whiff of the meat. After flipping the omelet in the pan, I bumped her out of my way with my hip and took the cookie sheet to set it on the counter. I pointed at the table and she went to sit back down, and began eating her toast again without argument. Sipping on the juice I brought her, she smiled at me before finishing her thought.

"Evan only has one of two bedrooms upstairs, silly." She laughed. "He's going to be building a house out on the back of our lot, plus he'll be on tour, so you can stay here with me."

"I'll think about it," I started.

"No thinking, you will."

"Fine, once they are headed out on tour, I will stay with you, but not before."

She nodded her approval. Once her breakfast was gone and I was finished putting everything for the guys in the containers she had left out on the counter, we quickly cleaned up our mess together. Grabbing the food and Avery's work bag, we made our way out to our vehicles.

"We'll have to take my car out to the lot, yours won't like it," she told me, heading toward her car.

I hopped in to move mine out of the way and get my own bags. After dropping the keys in the cup holder, should anyone need to move it, I got out and put my stuff in hers. While she backed up a bit, I noticed that there was indeed a road that branched off their driveway and headed around the side of their lot, and to the back wood line. It hadn't been there on their wedding day, just last week.

"Cooper and I have been talking about giving Evan a piece of land for some time," she told me, as we drove along the bumpy dirt. "The day after our wedding, Coop got the ball rolling. My dad and brother came in the next day and put in the temporary road."

"He doesn't have family around here like the others?" I asked, slightly confused.

"Nope," she replied sadly. "His mother was an absentee. She lives around here still, but they don't talk. He spent most of his teen years with the Hall family."

I was shocked, though it explained why Ave was so close to him. Evan was a sweet man, and I understood why many women were attracted to him. I had assumed he had come from a caring family like Cooper's to have ended up that way.

"I'll run this to them. You stay here," she said, pulling to a stop.

The men were busy putting stakes in the ground, stopping every little bit to look back at a set of plans on a piece of plywood supported by two sawhorses. A red pickup truck with the Grind logo was parked off to the side of the lot, and I could see Cooper's youngest brother, Rick, who was a foreman for the company, helping them. He flashed a grin at me in the car, along with a wave, and I returned it. Evan seemed to notice and quickly barked something at him I couldn't make out, that had Rick raising his arms and laughing. When Evan's eyes met mine through the glass, I glared and crossed my arms over my chest. The action caused him to smile and send me a wink. I rolled my eyes and waited as Avery gave her husband the bag of food before heading back to me.

"Wow!" She gasped as she sat down in her seat and shut the door. "That man has it bad for you."

"What are you talking about?" I questioned as she turned her SUV around and we headed to the office.

"Evan," she replied. "He just bit Rick's head off for waving to you."

"Eh, he'll find a new toy when he leaves on tour, and I'll be just a memory." I waved off her comment. I just hoped I could keep myself busy enough to forget about *him*.

EVAN

THE WOMAN WAS GOING TO drive me to drink, possibly literally. She tried to act indifferent around me, but I could see the way her body reacted to me. Her nipples would pebble under her prim clothes, her breathing would quicken, and her eyes would flash. She might have been able to keep her cheeks from turning that lovely shade of pink that I loved so much, yet she couldn't control it all. To others, Julie might have looked like the hard-ass professional that she wanted people to see, but I could see past that. She wanted me as bad as I wanted her. She just wasn't ready to give in.

Avery and Julie had worked late at the new office, not coming back to town until late in the evening. Julie had tried to rent a room at the local B&B, but Avery wouldn't hear of it. She made her friend feel bad enough that she had finally caved and agreed to stay with us. I had been on my best behavior, but not long after supper, she had retreated to the spare bedroom upstairs near mine to "work."

Knowing she would be sleeping right next door to me had my body on edge. I had finally given up trying to sleep around nine o'clock and changed into workout clothes. Sneaking downstairs so I didn't wake anyone else up, I crept into the basement. Cooper had soundproofed it to make sure that the clanging of the weights couldn't be heard in the house. I was grateful for that as I turned on the radio to a hard rock workout playlist on my phone and cranked it up.

I lost myself for the better part of an hour. Finishing up with free weights, I decided that another hour on the treadmill wouldn't hurt. I was just starting to feel tired, yet every time Julie's face popped into my head, I could feel an erection start to stir. What was it about her that had me so turned around and backwards? I had been with other women, had a few serious girlfriends, but none of them had sunk their claws in the way she had without even trying to. She didn't seem to want anything to do with me in the long run. Avery had kept pretty tight-lipped about that too. She wouldn't share a damn thing about Julie's current status with her husband, other than she wasn't wearing her ring and that they were separated.

I knew part of what drew me to her. She was gorgeous. Long wavy brown hair you wanted to run your fingers through, brown eyes you could get lost in, and a genuine smile that could melt a man when she actually showed it. Her brains were a whole other matter. The woman ran her own fucking business. According to Avery, Julie had taken the company over from her father full-time six years ago; prior to that, she had worked alongside him. They had fifteen employees at the Massachusetts location that managed approximately twenty businesses. The goal was to do the same in Maine. She was also very hands-on, from what I could see, and didn't rely on her employees to do all the work, putting in some extremely long hours.

When the treadmill kicked into cool down mode, I almost lost my footing. I was so engrossed in my thoughts, I hadn't realized I had already been running for over an hour. It was closing in on midnight, and my body finally seemed ready for sleep despite the fact that my brain was still busy. I cleaned up the equipment, grabbed a towel, and wiped my face down. Quietly making my way back upstairs, I was just pulling my shirt off when I felt small hands on my abs, followed by a gasp.

Looking down, I found Julie directly in front of me. The light from her room cast a glow over her and my cock sprang to life once again. Cursing under my breath, I held still. She must have been coming out just as I was coming up the stairs and because I couldn't see her, I had almost run her over. She was wearing boy shorts and a tiny t-shirt where the hem barely reached the top of her underwear. Vanilla filled my nostrils and I let out a groan. Her eyes were hooded and she licked her lips as she ran her hands down my abs, tracing over each of the bumps in the muscles. She only stopped when she reached the top of my athletic shorts.

Grabbing her hands in mine just as they started to dip into the waistband at my hip, I let out another strangled curse. I moved swiftly and had her up against the wall, her hands above her head clasped in mine and my leg between hers, before she could react. I knew that once she realized what she was doing, she would back off again. It was time for me to let her know I wasn't giving up on her that easily.

"What did I tell you before about playing with fire, boss lady?" I growled, feeling the heat of her core against my knee.

"I...I...I'm sorry," she stuttered, pulling on her hands, her eyes wide when her lust-filled brain started to clear.

"Don't ever apologize for touching me," I said, gentling my voice when I felt her stiffen.

"I shouldn't have done that," she replied.

Her head tilted up with the comment and her voice became stronger. I could see her walls going back up, one by one. Not giving her a chance to fight it, I pulled my leg back and immediately placed my body against hers, hip to toe. I knew by the flash in her eyes that she could feel my erection against her belly, and by the hitch in her breath, she was just as affected by me as I was by her. I leaned in, running my nose up her throat, and inhaled. The smell I had learned to associate with her was there and had my lips parting in a smile.

"You can touch me whenever you want," I whispered in her ear, then grazed my teeth over the spot just behind it, causing her to buck against me. "If I didn't think you would regret it in the morning, I would drag you back to my room and remind you of how good we were together."

"I don't think…"

"But," I interrupted her, "we are going to take this slow."

"We are, are we?" she questioned.

Her tone caused my smile to widen. I licked and nipped down the column of her throat and around to the front of her collarbone. Her fighting against my hands had seized and her breathing was now coming in shallow pants. I could almost bet that if I put my hands inside those little shorts, I would find her wet and ready for me. The thought had me rubbing my cock against her, wishing the layers of cotton were gone. This time, when she let out a small sigh, I covered her mouth with mine.

Julie tried with all her might to fight me physically, but the moment my lips touched hers, she caved. They parted to let my tongue in and as soon as she did, I backed off the pace. I lazily stroked mine against hers, twirling slightly when she pressed her hips against me. When I couldn't take any more of the teasing myself, I pulled my mouth slowly away and rested my forehead against hers.

"Tomorrow morning, eight o'clock, we're going to breakfast," I told her. "You owe me."

Giving her one more chaste kiss, I backed away and let her go. She seemed stunned at first that I had released her, but quickly recovered and scurried back into the room she had come from. The door shut with a defiant *click*, and I chuckled as I adjusted myself. Athletic shorts did nothing to hide a raging hard-on. So much for working out.

Sleep eluded me that night, and by seven o'clock the next morning, I was making my way down the stairs, carrying my cowboy boots so I didn't wake anyone. The cold shower I had taken helped little with the pain radiating from the worst case of blue balls I'd ever had. I would continue to take things slow to warm Julie up to the idea of us, but damn, I was only going to be able to take care of myself so many times. Her warmth wrapped around me, sucking me dry, was going to have to happen sooner rather than later.

"Well, I guess I didn't need to worry about waking anyone up." I laughed when I entered the kitchen and found Avery dancing around making breakfast.

"Geez, Evan!" she shrieked, putting her hand over her heart. "Give me a heart attack, why don't ya?"

"Sorry, sweetheart," I apologized with a grin, moving to place a kiss on the top of her head. "No breakfast for me or Julie, I'm taking her out."

"Oh?" she asked, perking back up.

I didn't get a chance to answer her before Cooper came in like a whirlwind, totally bypassing me for his wife. He grabbed her, bringing her against him roughly, and kissing her long and deep. I coughed, turning my head to sit and put my boots on. If I watched them too much longer, I would have to go back upstairs and rub one out. Hearing soft steps on the stairs, I looked and saw Julie just clearing the last one with her bags in her hands. I smiled widely, knowing she had hoped to scoot out and miss our meal.

"Evan!" Cooper boomed, bringing my attention back to my best friend and his wife.

He stood with one arm around her shoulders, grinning like an idiot. I raised an eyebrow at him. I saw him moving his free hand, only to realize he was circling it on Avery's belly. My eyes shot up to her face to find her cheeks flush, and a matching smile on her lips. They were going to have a baby. Jumping up with a *"Whoop!"* I brought them into a group hug. I couldn't have been happier for them.

I felt, rather than saw, Julie moving toward the door behind me. Cooper must have caught her as well because he released us and made his way to her in three strides. Surprising everyone, he picked her up and whirled her around. The look on her face started as one of horror, but quickly softened, and she wrapped her arms around his neck, laughing. I felt my heart skip a beat. Avery squeezed my arm and when I looked down at her, she tilted her head in their direction.

"Coop," I warned, a smile playing on my lips. "That one's mine."

I watched as he chuckled and set her back on her feet. He didn't let her go right away, which had me watching them closely. There were whispered words and a sweet kiss to her forehead from him before he finally stepped back. I felt my gut clench at the intimacy of it, now I knew how he felt when I joked with Avery. Cooper stopped when he got to me and put his hands on my shoulders.

"Fight for that one," he said, low enough for my ears only.

I nodded, dumbfounded. Julie quickly composed herself and reached for her bags again. I had already snapped out of my stupor and had them by the handles before she could get her hands on them. She narrowed her eyes at me, a look she seemed to have perfected, yet I threw her a grin and led the way out the door. Putting her bags in her backseat, I closed the car door and grabbed her hand before she could get in.

"You're riding with me," I informed her, leaving little room for argument when I led her to my truck.

"That's just stupid," she snapped, trying to tug her hand free. "I can just leave from the restaurant."

"I'm going to take every second with you I can get."

She stopped and her mouth gaped. It seemed I had finally rendered her speechless. Knowing it wouldn't last long, I opened the passenger door of my truck and put my hands on her hips to help her in. It didn't have a huge lift, but it was enough that even with the bars, a woman had to pull herself up to get into it. The smile never left my face as I made my way around the front of the Dodge.

The ride to the restaurant was quiet, not that I expected much different. Julie was still fighting this thing between us with all she had. Even if we had a short-term relationship, which wasn't my endgame, why couldn't it be enjoyable? Why exactly was she so gun-shy? The divorce, maybe? I snuck a glance at her just before I turned into the parking lot and found her looking out the window. The lines of her face were relaxed until she noticed where we were, then the walls were back.

The Full Belly was already bustling. It was a good-sized diner that had recently reopened after a major renovation. The owner, Morgan Kramer, had purchased the business from her aging aunt a few years ago, and it hadn't taken long for her to realize that it needed some upgrades. When we stepped inside, I nodded in approval. She had kept the vintage look, but now everything was clean and shining in the sunlight that streamed in through the large windows. The long bar that sat on the right had bar stools that looked like they were right out of an old soda shop, and a register sat on the end closest to the door. Booths lined the walls and a scattering of tables were in the middle of the room, most of which were already filled.

"Hey, handsome!" came a greeting from behind the bar.

I turned and found Morgan pouring coffee into a customer's cup. Her wavy blonde tresses were in a messy bun on top of her head while her blue eyes were sparkling. The curves under the fitted "My belly is full, is yours?" t-shirt would catch any man's eye, as would the ass I knew was tucked into the tight jeans she was sporting.

"Hi, gorgeous," I replied. "Can we sit anywhere?"

"Yep, help yourself and one of us will be right over."

I had to bite my lip to keep from laughing when I felt Julie stiffen over our exchange. Putting my hand on her back, I steered her toward a corner booth I saw was empty. She went willingly, yet her back was ramrod straight again. Oh, this was going to be interesting.

"Did you bring me here just to show off your girlfriend?" she finally snapped as she settled herself into the seat across from me.

The minute the words left her mouth, I knew she regretted them. Her cheeks turned that cute shade of pink and she quickly hid behind one of the menus that was already on the table. I let out a slight chuckle that earned me a glare over the top of the plastic-covered paper. Coughing, I tried unsuccessfully to cover it up, along with my growing grin. She was jealous. All hope was not lost.

"Hi there," Morgan greeted as she came to a stop at our table. Turning over my coffee cup and filling it, she gestured to Julie. With a flip of her own cup, my companion pushed it toward her.

"Morgan, this is Julie, Avery's business partner," I introduced, leaning back slightly to watch Julie.

"Oh! It's so nice to finally meet you!" Morgan exclaimed. "Avery has told me so much about you!"

"Umm...thanks," Julie murmured, confusion all over her face.

"Avery and Morgan were friends in high school and went to college together. They both have their MBAs," I supplied, enjoying the show.

Julie's eyes snapped up to Morgan, who wore a warm smile, then back to me. She hadn't expected that one. The childish part of me wanted to keep dragging this out and to push more of her buttons just to see her brown eyes light up, but I was getting hungry and I was smart enough to know when to stop.

"Can I get a Hungry Man?" I asked, turning my attention back to the shop owner.

"Yes, sir," she said, writing on the pad in her hand. "And you, darling?"

"I'll take a western omelet with a side of bacon."

When my old friend left the table, I put all my focus back on Julie. She was still ruffled from the conversation with Morgan and busied herself with preparing her coffee, never looking up at me. The stirring seemed to go on forever after she had put a single packet of creamer and two sugars into her mug. Finally, I put my finger on her chin and lifted her face so I could see her eyes. There were a hundred emotions raging behind them.

"I meant what I said last night," I told her softly. "We'll take this slow."

"I'm not going to be another notch in your bedpost," she whispered.

Ah, so that was what this was all about. She thought I was just out for the conquest. I guess I was going to have to convince her otherwise.

"That's not what is going on here," I said simply.

"Isn't it?" she asked, jerking her chin from my grasp. "You could have any woman in this place, including the one that was just at this table. I'm a little more of a challenge because I'm Avery's business partner and I'm a bitch."

I wasn't surprised at the sass, but the tone behind it had more of a bite than I had heard from her before. It made me wonder what exactly her ex had done to her, and it also made me want to punch the fucker in the face for breaking her heart.

"Morgan and I have been friends since we were in high school, and I've never had feelings for her that way. As for you being a bitch, that is still up for discussion," I joked, throwing her a grin and flashing my dimples; the mood needed to be lightened.

The laugh that escaped her surprised her so much that she slapped her hand over her mouth. She had wanted to stay mad at me. I wasn't about to let that happen. I knew she was softer under that tough exterior than anyone knew. The night of the wedding, I had seen a side that I'm sure not many got to see. She had been relaxed and responsive in every way. I just needed to remind her of that. I pulled her hand away from her lips and watched as she slowly eased her shoulders down. After squeezing her hand, I released it and took a sip of my coffee.

"Oh, and Evan?" She smirked from behind her cup, causing my eyebrows to lift. "I'm not yours."

JULIE

I THINK I HAD RUN more in the past two weeks than I had in years. Sure, it had become a regular part of my routine, but now I was doing it twice a day and for longer. My quick two-mile runs had turned into four miles. I had to, though; if I didn't, I was going to gain weight. I couldn't stop eating. Damn stress.

My phone *dinged*, signaling a message, and I groaned before reaching for it. I was sitting on the couch in my office, papers spread out around me, trying to get myself organized for meetings with two possible new clients for the Maine office. Along with their financials was a stack of resumes for accountants and office personnel. Swiping my finger across the screen, I tried not to smile when I saw Evan's name pop up. The man had been incorrigible.

> **E: Whatcha doin', boss lady?**

J: Working

I had tried keeping things light and simple with my messages, but he hadn't gotten the hint nor had he stopped sending them. As much as I wanted *not* to get involved, the man made me laugh. The good looks were such a small piece of him. He was tender, caring, and knew the right things to say to make a bad day better. I was struggling to keep him at arm's length.

E: You do that too much

J: Part of running your own business

E: Have you eaten yet?

What was it with this man and feeding me? Though I really couldn't complain about our last meal together. While it started a bit awkward, thanks to a little bit of jealousy, it had ended up being very enjoyable. Our conversation had flowed into business talk. Evan had asked about Lane & Son, genuinely seeming interested, and I had been more than happy to oblige.

Had I eaten yet? It seemed like that was all I had done lately. The stress of the business and trying to keep my thoughts of a certain bassist out of my mind had me turning to food. Potato chips, chocolate, and ice cream were just a few of my go-tos. Kelly had started teasing me when I brought in a candy jar and placed it on my desk, fully stocked with Reese's Peanut Butter Cups and mini Twix bars.

J: Not yet. Wow, hadn't realized it was so late.

I really hadn't. The screen showed 6:40 p.m. Everyone else in the office was long gone. A vague memory of Kelly letting me

THE UNKNOWN | 47

know she was leaving and locking the door behind her came to mind. What time had that been? Shrugging, I put my phone back down on the coffee table and got up to stretch. Just as I was bending over to do my hamstrings, a noise out front startled me, nearly sending face first into my carpet.

Before I could gather my wits, I caught a whiff of Chinese food. Shaking my head, I straightened and was about to make my way out of my office when I heard footsteps and rustling bags. I didn't have time to be scared because right along with the smell of the food was the aroma of a cologne I knew all too well. How the hell?

"You really do work too much, you know," he teased the minute he stepped over the threshold and put the bags down on my conference room table.

I watched him, unable to speak. I was pissed that he was here; he certainly wasn't taking my hints. Yet, a piece of me was also happy to see him, touched that he wanted to take care of and fuss over me. Before I could move toward him, Evan turned and weaved around the papers to reach me. Stopping so we were only an inch apart, he tucked a loose hair behind my ear and ran his fingertips back across my cheek. When he reached my lips, he brought my bottom one down with his thumb and placed his fingers beneath my chin to hold me in place.

"Hi," he whispered, his breath causing me to shiver.

"Hi," I responded just as softly, fighting the urge to close my eyes in surrender.

After taking me in for a few moments, he leaned down and ran his tongue over the lip he still held captive. I sighed when he released it and moved to cup my cheeks. The kiss was sweet; just a brush of his lips against mine. Our bodies didn't touch in any way. I felt the passion behind it all the way to my toes.

"Let's clean this up so we can get some food in ya," he said, when he finally broke away.

I had to keep myself from swaying toward him when he let my face go and started moving piles. Slapping his hands away, I pointed to the table where the food was. He chuckled, leaving me to my papers. It may have looked like chaos, but in reality, I knew where everything was. Making quick work of putting everything back in the files where they belonged, I moved them to my credenza and had to stifle a groan when my stomach started to roll with a hunger I hadn't realized had been there. The sound it made earned a chuckle from Evan and I had to smile in return.

"Okay, how did you get in?" I asked, once we were settled back on the couch with open containers spread out on the coffee table in front of us.

"I may have had an accomplice," he admitted, taking a bite of the chicken finger he had just dipped in duck sauce.

"Oh?" I raised an eyebrow.

"Sorry." He apologized with one of his smiles that sent his dimples winking at me. "I can't give away all my secrets."

I laughed. It could only have been one of two people, Kelly or Avery. I certainly couldn't get mad at either of them; after all, they were just looking out for me. They weren't making this *keep away from Evan* thing any easier though.

We were quiet while we ate, but it wasn't awkward. It felt comfortable. My bare feet were tucked under me, leaning my body toward him and he sat back like he belonged here. His hair was hidden under a backwards Red Sox hat, while his body was covered completely in a baggy hooded sweatshirt and well-worn jeans. It didn't matter what he wore, though, the man was gorgeous. I stopped mid-chew when his baby blues turned and caught me staring at him. He just winked and went back to his food.

"So, you traveled all the way here just to have dinner with me?" I questioned. It seemed too good to be true.

"Well, no," he confessed, setting his plate down and turning to me.

I felt my stomach clench and my eyes narrowed at him. I knew it. He thought he was going to get in my pants. Boy, did he have another thing coming to him. What the hell had I been thinking, beginning to soften to him? He was just like the rest of them.

"I figured we could get a little make-out time in here at the office. Then, I would follow you home to make sure you got there safely. After that, I'll head back."

"What?" I stammered.

"I told you before, and I will tell you as many times as you need to hear it," he said quietly, brushing his fingertips down my arm. "We will take this slow."

"You keep saying that," I snapped, "but all I hear is that you have the patience of a saint until you go back out on tour. Then, I'll just be another pretty face."

"Damn it, Julie!" he roared. "I mean what I say, how the hell can I get that through to you! Do you want the guys to take pictures and videos of me when we get back out there, so you can keep tabs on me? Do you want to GPS my phone so you can track me? I'm a man that is true to my word."

I was taken back. I had never heard or seen Evan act like that before. He was always so soft-spoken and happy-go-lucky. His face was red and he pulled his hat off to run his fingers through his hair, only to slam it back down. Letting his head fall into his hands, he took some long deep breaths in and out to calm himself.

"I'm sorry," he apologized, sometime later. "You seem to be one of two people that can cause me to lose my shit."

"Good to know, especially considering you are one of the few men that can seem to get under my skin."

His eyes came up and met mine. They were calm again and the smile he always had was back. I returned his with one of my own. He wasn't like the others, yet I still couldn't bring myself to trust him completely. I couldn't even understand how Avery did it; hell, she knew Cooper better than I knew Evan. Knew he had been with plenty of women while he had been on the road without her for years.

"I want to try this," Evan let me know, shifting so that his hip was against my knees and putting an arm around the back of the couch. "We have too much chemistry not to."

"I'm not going to argue the fact that the sex was good," I told him, causing him to raise an eyebrow and smirk. "Okay, it was the best I've ever had, but that isn't all a relationship is about."

"Fully aware, boss lady," he agreed. "That's why I said we would take this slow. We will get to know each other better. It's not like we are complete strangers."

It was true. We had known each other for the better part of a year and we had already had sex. Wonderful, mind-blowing sex that had my body heating and my nipples perking beneath my off-white cotton three-quarter length V-neck sweater that I had paired with my brown dress pants that morning. Evan's gaze dropped down and his lips curved when he saw my body responding. Licking them and moving his eyes back up, I noticed that they had turned a darker shade of blue.

"Evan," I warned, putting a hand out to rest on his chest as he moved toward me.

"Slow," he repeated.

His free hand came around to cup my cheek just as his lips met mine. It was tender. The sweetness of it all made me sigh and he again used the opportunity to slide his tongue into my mouth and against mine. None of it was rushed and despite my hand fisting in his sweatshirt, Evan didn't change the pace. He stroked and twirled his tongue in ways that left me wondering how it would feel against my clit, or moving in and out of me. My panties started to dampen and my core throbbed at the thought. Moving slowly, so he didn't stop me, I wrapped my arms around his neck and slid to straddle him. Our mouths never parted.

Evan's hands moved to my hips while I got comfortable and then slid tantalizingly around to cup my ass gently. The kissing continued to be steady and unrushed, though the rest of our body parts were begging for more. I felt his erection through the light cotton of my pants and I rocked against him, using the same pace that he had set with our mouths. His hands flexed against my butt and shifted to help with the motion reminiscent of an old rocking chair.

I felt the orgasm building. There was no way that I was going to come like some horny teenager. I wanted him inside me. I wanted to squeeze him with my inner walls as I rode him. I braced myself and tried to ward off the feeling. Evan's hands gripped my ass a little tighter, and with a slight shift to his hips, he started pushing against me as he brought me down harder.

"Evan!" I cried against his lips, fighting the urge.

"Let go, baby," he whispered against my lips. "Just let go."

So I did. Grabbing his shoulders, I threw my head back and let it out. It was so strong that I could feel the muscles in my legs shaking as Evan continued to thrust his hips up to push his erection against my clit. When I couldn't take it anymore, I brought my head forward and immediately tucked it against his neck, wrapping my arms around him tightly. I was mortified. Only unexperienced women who didn't know how to control their bodies did what I just did.

Now, I had to figure out how to get off him and get him out of here without looking him in the face. He was more than happy to hold me; I'm not even sure how long we sat like that. The only thing I noticed was the room had started to get darker, and the couple lamps that were on began to cast shadows onto the walls. When I felt his hands making their way toward my face, I bit down on his shoulder to keep him from moving it.

"Ouch." He chuckled. "Let me look at you."

"Why?" I snapped, letting him cradle my face and looking into his eyes.

They weren't judging or pitying. They were warm and sparkling as always, though darker with what I assumed was lust, since his erection kept dancing against my core, looking for its own release. I felt my cheeks grow warm with embarrassment and I dropped my eyes.

"Hey," he coaxed, dipping his head to try to keep our eyes connected. "You haven't been with a lot of men, have you?"

"No," I mumbled, only answering because he didn't ask to judge, but to understand.

"Julie," he pleaded, the tone causing me to snap my head up. "We will do this slow. I promise."

EVAN

"WHAT THE HELL ARE YOU doing?" I heard Cooper ask, breaking me from my trance.

"Huh?"

"You're about ready to pour coffee into your cereal, dude," he said with a chuckle.

Shaking my head, I looked down. Sure enough, I was about to pour my whole coffee mug into my bowl rather than the milk sitting in the jug in front of me. Sighing, I put down my cup and reached for the milk instead.

"You've got it bad," he commented, sitting down across from me, sipping from his coffee.

"I'm not sure if I've got it bad, or if the case of blue balls I have is affecting my brain," I muttered.

"What was that?" he asked, perking up with a smile.

"Nothing," I replied, shaking my head.

"Good morning, gentlemen," Avery greeted as she entered. "Are you all ready for today?"

"I am," I admitted, leaning over to wrap my arm around her waist and pull her to my side. God love the woman who could change the subject just when I needed her to.

She laughed, leaning over to kiss the top of my head, and wiggled away before Coop could wrangle her from my arms into his lap. I chuckled at her squeal and his scowling face. While I would miss the two of them when I did move into my own place, it would be nice to let them have their alone time. Today was the day we finally got started on the footers for my house. The groundwork had already been done.

Everything seemed to be expedited, and had my head spinning. Paperwork had been signed left and right, plans drafted and changed and drafted again. Grind had been in and out, and it was all on schedule to be completed by the time we returned from our tour in December. The entire band would be as active in the build as we could be until we left in just a few short weeks. Now, I just had to convince a certain someone to oversee it all while we were gone.

"Wakey, wakey!" Rick boomed as he came banging through the kitchen door. "Time to get to work."

I laughed when Cooper flinched at his brother's chipper attitude, and almost doubled over when he swatted at him when Rick grabbed Avery around the waist and planted a loud smacking kiss on her lips. Cooper muttered something about not needing a younger brother as he got up to pull his wife into his arms, resting his hands on her still flat stomach.

"You would miss me," Rick informed him as he helped himself to a cup of coffee and nodded at me. "You ready, man?"

"To supervise," I joked, finishing my breakfast. "These hands are my life."

"They are for all of us, you jackass," Cooper argued.

"Yeah, but I make the best sound," I retorted with a smirk, getting up to put my bowl in the sink.

"That may be the case, but you couldn't sound like you do without me," came Matt's voice from the doorway.

Our banter with Rick had drowned out the noises of Chris and Matt tromping into the house. Both of them had been staying with their families ever since Coop and Ave had tied the knot; neither of them could bring themselves to purchase anything in Maine yet. The battle of Matt and I had been a never-ending one, a long-standing joke.

"Maybe so, but I'm the better-looking one," I reminded him, flashing a smile.

"Says the guy that had to jerk himself off this morning," Matt shot back.

"And you didn't?" I retorted with a snicker.

The sound of a feminine clearing of the throat behind Chris had us all turning toward the kitchen door. Julie stood there with a faint smile; she was fighting the full-blown version, and was dressed professional as always. She wore a black blazer over a bright pink top, black dress pants, and bright pink heels. Her hair was bunched into a tight bun at the back of her head that had my hands itching to pull it down and run my fingers through it. Those brown pools that immediately had my dick pushing against my jeans, were sparkling with a hint of mirth. Slowly, she was starting to loosen up with us.

"Are you ready, Avery?" she asked, gesturing outside with a tip of her head.

"Gosh, yes," Ave replied, pushing away from her husband after giving him a quick kiss. "Get me away from all of this testosterone."

"I'm hurt." I feigned chest pain, placing my hand over my heart.

"Oh, stop it," she teased, putting her hand on my stomach and going up on tiptoes to kiss my cheek, earning a growl from Coop. "Have fun today."

"She loves me more, man," I shot at my friend, moving to try to get my hands on Julie before she left.

"Freeze, Foster," she stated, putting the hand out that wasn't holding her keys. "I have a meeting with a potential client and I don't want you to wrinkle me."

I stopped and had to keep my mouth from dropping open. Her lips were slightly tipped at the corners and there was a definite teasing tone to her voice. The guys behind me all snickered and let out *oohhhs* behind me. Her cheeks flushed pink with the calls, but she held her ground. I flashed her the grin with the dimples and saw her breath hitch.

"Let's go." She motioned to Avery, who had grabbed her work bag and met her at the door, and was still holding her hand out to keep me at bay.

"Bye, ladies," Rick chirped, stepping in front of me.

The women left and surprisingly enough, the guys didn't start in on me. As soon as we had heard Julie's car start, Rick had whipped out the floor plans and laid them on the kitchen table. We all gathered around and discussed the changes that had been made. I was opting for a simple Cape, with three bedrooms, two bathrooms, and a mudroom to connect the house with a three-bay garage. It wasn't much different from Cooper and Avery's—the master bedroom and bath would be downstairs, and the other bath and two bedrooms would be upstairs. It would also have a gorgeous farmers porch.

The smile never left my face as we rolled them back up and all made our way outside to a couple of the trucks. Piling in, we made the short trek to my piece of property. Every time I stepped foot on it and looked toward Coop's place, I felt like I was home. It wasn't a feeling that came easy to me, given my childhood. Even our place in Nashville never really felt like "home." Yet, this little piece of property, the fifteen acres I had been given, was doing it before the structure was even on it.

"So, how are things going with Julie?" Chris finally asked as

Rick and Coop worked to make sure everything was level before we started setting the footers.

"Just fine," I replied nonchalantly. I didn't want to give away anything. They didn't need to know that she was fairly innocent in the bedroom, though our first night together had been no indicator.

"Bullshit!" Coop hollered from his position in the hole. "What was that you were muttering about blue balls this morning?"

All eyes turned on me. I was going to fucking kill him. I knew how to get myself out of this mess, and they wouldn't second guess me, but it wouldn't sit well with Julie if she heard about it. Shaking my head, I got up and looked down at him. His face showed no signs of remorse; instead, it held a shit-eating grin. Payback was a bitch.

"You know how it is, Coop," I reminded him. "Going from all those women to just one. Especially since I told her we would go slow. Just taking the boys a little time to adjust, that's all."

His face was priceless. The other guys laughed like hyenas and I couldn't help but grin myself. He had become mute about his sex life since he and Avery had gotten back together. Other than the fact that we had often heard them and saw him groping her more times than we could count, we knew nothing. My little comment was a quick jab that let him know I wouldn't be any different with boss lady. I wouldn't be sharing her with anyone.

I couldn't say that I was as reserved in the bedroom as Julie; however, I certainly hadn't been as much of a dog on the road as some of my bandmates. I'd had a few relationships and those were the women that had shared my bed, not the groupies that hung out after the shows.

Now, I still had to convince her that I would be loyal once I got on the road. While she had seemed to relax a little since our encounter in her office earlier on in the week, she hadn't been answering my text messages or calls. Whether it was embarrassment or fear of getting attached, I wasn't sure.

It looked like the time leading up to our leaving on tour would be full of interesting things. Between the house and Julie, I was going to have my hands full. For the first time in my life, I was finding my own way and I wasn't looking forward to going back on the road. I had a feeling I knew exactly how Coop now felt when he had to leave Avery. It was time to get my life in order.

JULIE

T HIS MAN. WHAT WAS IT about him that caused me to go against everything I had ever believed in? Independent. That's how I had been raised. My parents had instilled in me from an early age that I could do anything and everything for myself. I didn't need a man. Maybe that's why it had been so easy with Ryan; he hadn't done anything for me. Evan, on the other hand, wanted to do everything for me, dote on me.

And yet, here I was, driving to Maine again. Thank God my car got great gas mileage because the two-and-a-half-hour drive was becoming as common a drive as the one to the home office. I took a deep breath and forced myself to relax into my seat as I watched the tail lights of the truck in front me. I had to remind myself this trip wasn't for work, it was personal. The guys would be leaving tomorrow and, after a rather long battle with myself, I realized I couldn't let the night go by without seeing him. The uncertainty of what would happen once I saw him gnawed at me, but for once in my life, I was going to go with the flow. There would be no planning, no guarantees.

Unfortunately, because I had fought with myself for so long, the sun had started to set as I had hit the road. It was already nearing ten o'clock and I was beyond mad for waiting as long as I did. I had texted Avery to let her know I was coming, but told her not to tell Evan. She assured me that he would be happy to see me. She also let me know she would leave the front door unlocked, and not to worry about her and Coop because they would be locked away in their room, enjoying their last night together for a while.

When I pulled in to the long drive, I let out a shaky breath. Nerves were starting to set in, but there was no turning back now. The house was dark as I approached, only a small light on what I assumed was the stove casting a glow in the kitchen window. I stopped my car behind Evan's truck and killed the ignition. Putting a hand on my belly to try to calm the butterflies, I inhaled and exhaled a few times. This was it. All or nothing.

Before I could question anything else, I grabbed my overnight bag and climbed out. Quietly, I opened the door and locked it when I shut it behind me. There was soft music playing from somewhere in the house. Making my way through the house and to the stairs, I started my way up. A light burned at the top, showing me the way, and I was surprised to find Evan's door open. He was nowhere to be seen when I poked my head in though. The lamp on his bedside table was on, and I could see a pair of jeans and a tank top thrown on the end of the bed. I put my bag down and grabbed my phone.

> *J: What are you doing on your last night at home?*

E: Burning some energy so I can sleep since you wouldn't let me come visit you. 😊

J: How are you doing that if you aren't with me? 😊

E: My favorite activity other than sex with you 😊 *Lifting.*

J: What did I tell you about those candid comments?

E: Boss lady, I'm not one to give up that easily 😊

Well, that answered that question. He was in the basement. I looked at myself in his mirror quickly before I made my way back downstairs. My brown hair hung down my back in waves and my face was naked. No makeup, no jewelry. Tonight, he was getting Julie in her simplest form. The woman that no one else got to see. I slipped off my sandals and tiptoed back to the kitchen. The basement door was closed, and when I opened it, music blared up the stairwell.

Evan had 90's rock on. I couldn't make out the song, yet the steady pumping seemed to be going right along with my heart. As I made my way down, I could hear the sounds of him putting the bar back on the rack with a *clink*. I reached the bottom and rounded the corner. His muscled back was to me and he was gloriously sweaty. He had opted to lift without a shirt and his athletic shorts rode low on his hips, showcasing the two dimples just above his ass. My breath caught. His tattoos seemed to be brighter and the veins all over his body were straining from his exertions. After adjusting his gloves, he bent over to retrieve another weight to add to the bar, and I sucked in a breath when his shorts grew snug around his backside.

Somehow Evan heard the noise and it startled him. He dropped the weight and whipped around. The minute his eyes met mine, he instantly relaxed, and the smile that he was known for took over. I couldn't stop my lips from turning up in response. Walking to him, I clasped my hands in front of myself to keep from reaching for him.

"Hey," I greeted when I stopped in front of him, close enough that I could feel the heat coming from his body.

"Hey," he returned, pulling off his gloves and reaching out to tuck some of my hair behind my ear. "I thought you had work you wanted to get done?"

"Yeah, well, there was something that was a little more important," I told him softly.

"Something or someone?" he asked, his voice going deep and low, caressing my skin just like his finger that now ran down my neck and around to my collarbone.

"Both," I replied, finally releasing my hands and bringing them up to put them on his hips.

"Thank fuck," he murmured.

Evan brought his hand up that had been just about to dip down my cleavage and cupped the back of my head, as the other went to my hip to pull our bodies flush against each other. I moaned when I felt his erection, strong and hard, through the thin layers of cotton. He swallowed the noise and slanted his mouth over mine, taking the kiss hot and demanding right from the start. The little bit strip of fabric between my legs was instantly wet. This was why I was here—this man made me forget everything else in the world.

"Hold on," I panted, my fingers digging into his bare skin.

"How about you hold on?" he groaned, his hands coming down and around to grip my ass and pull me up to wrap my legs around him.

When he realized that I had on a thong, much different from

my normal wear, he growled. I wrapped my arms around his neck as he moved us to the weight bench and sat down. The sweat from his workout soaked through my dress, but I didn't care, especially when I could easily feel every muscle from the lack of clothing. He kissed his way down my neck and nipped when he reached my shoulder, bringing the strap of my dress down with his teeth.

"Are you trying to torment me, boss lady?" he asked. "No bra, tiny panties."

"I thought it would make you happy," I said on a sigh as he kissed his way back over my collarbone and down to my cleavage.

"Very happy," he murmured, pushing down on my hips to grind his length against my core. "Can't you tell?"

"Oh, yes," I moaned. "But we need to talk first."

It was half-hearted and he knew it. Pulling the straps the rest of the way down with one hand, Evan steadied my back with the other. When my breasts were bared to him, his mouth instantly found my right nipple and nipped at it. I wrapped my legs tighter around his lower back and rocked against him in response. My clit pulsed against his straining erection, and I didn't know how much longer I would last.

"We will talk later, Julie," he informed me, biting my nipple and then latching on to suck. "I promise."

The use of my full name sent chills down my spine. I wasn't going to argue; I couldn't, because all the blood from my brain was currently pooling in my lower extremities. I dug my nails into his shoulders and hissed when he switched sides of my chest. His blue eyes came up to meet mine as I watched him and felt his tongue toying with my nipple in his mouth.

"I need to be in you, *now*," he growled. "Are you still on the pill? I don't have anything down here."

"Yes, I am," I gasped.

Shifting one arm under my ass, he used the other to pull his shorts and boxers down in one motion. He had barely done that before he was lining up the tip of his dick with my entrance.

Moving my underwear with his finger, he thrust in quickly, and I gasped at the intrusion. He wasn't a small man and filled me as he bottomed out.

"Fuck, you're tight," he moaned. "Tighter than I remember. I'm not going to last long, baby."

"Me either," I assured him, wrapping my legs and arms tighter around him. "Hard and fast."

"You don't have to tell me twice," he growled.

Evan's hands gripped my ass and pulled me up and down his member just the way I had requested, hard and fast. Four strokes in and my inner walls were tightening around him as I felt my orgasm take over. I moaned loud and long as I let go, and the noises had him coming with me.

"Julie," he ground out as he pumped up, slapping his pelvis against mine.

"Evan," I cried, the sweet pain almost becoming too much.

All movement slowly seized, and the only sounds that could be heard were our pants as our labored breathing started to calm. Our foreheads rested together and we were still intimately connected. Every few seconds, I could feel his dick twitch inside me and I would clench around him. My body wasn't done, and by the feel of his still semi-hard erection, neither was he. It had been just as good as I remembered it from the wedding.

Pulling away slightly so that he could look at me, Evan flashed his killer smile, dimples and all, before asking, "How the hell are we going to get upstairs like this?"

EVAN

I OPENED MY EYES RELUCTANTLY. The sun was just starting to rise and gorgeous yellows, oranges, and pinks filled the sky outside my window. Looking down, I sighed with contentment. Julie's head rested on my pec, and her arm, along with her leg, were across my body. I held the hand of the arm that was flung over my body in my hand against my heart. Her body was warm against mine and her vanilla fragrance wafted to my nostrils. The blood started to pool in my loins just from the feel and smell of her.

"How long are you going to watch me sleep?" came the drowsy voice.

"As long as you'll let me," I told her, kissing her head and maneuvering us so that she was under me.

I braced myself on my elbows and tucked one of my legs between her smooth ones. Her hair was partially spread out around her, causing me to tuck my fingers into it so I could play with it rather than grope her, which was what I really wanted to do. Her eyes were starting to wake and I felt her fingers making paths back and forth across my hips.

"What did you want to talk about last night?" I asked, leaning to drop a quick kiss on her nose.

Her hands stilled and her body stiffened slightly. When her eyes dropped, so did my stomach. It couldn't have been all that bad considering she had come to me, right? Especially after she had repeatedly pushed me away at every turn. I used one finger to lift her chin so our eyes could meet, and I brushed my lips across hers briefly.

"You can talk to me about anything, Julie," I reminded her.

"I know." She sighed. "I wanted to tell you about what went wrong with Ryan."

"Your ex?"

"Almost ex, but yeah." She cringed. "He isn't exactly making the divorce process easy."

"Okay, what happened?" I asked, moving my hand back to play with her hair, trying to keep things light.

"He went to Vegas for a business trip, just before Cooper and Avery's wedding," she started. "I guess that alone should have tipped me off."

"Not everyone that goes there abides by the 'what happens in Vegas, stays in Vegas' mentality," I told her with a grin.

"True, but that wasn't the case with him. I went to surprise him —we hadn't exactly seen much of each other because of our crazy schedules. I had thought things were going really well, well enough that I wanted to let him know I was ready to start a family."

"I'm not liking where this is going," I grumbled, moving one hand to cup her cheek.

"I had the hotel manager open the door to the suite and I found him in the living room, with his secretary bent over the arm of the chair. They hadn't even heard me come in and were going at it like rabbits," she whispered, turning her face into my palm so she could kiss it.

"Oh, baby," I said, my voice low and soothing, "I'm so sorry."

"It nearly crushed me, Evan." Her voice cracked.

"That's why you've been pushing me away?" I asked, wiping a stray tear away that rolled down her cheek.

"Yes, I'm scared that I am just a conquest for you, and that when you get out on the road, you'll just forget me. You're a handsome man, and it wouldn't take much for you to woo someone else into your bed."

"You think I'm handsome?" I joked, my eyebrows shooting up in mock surprise.

"You know you are, you goof." She giggled, slapping me lightly on the side.

"It may be easy for me to find another woman, so to speak," I told her, all humor gone, "but I don't *want* another woman. I want you, only you."

"If I give you my heart, Evan, can you promise me you won't break it?" Julie pleaded, her voice quiet and breaking on the last word.

"I can promise you that I will try like hell not to, and if I do, it won't be on purpose," I vowed.

She sighed heavily and closed her eyes. More tears escaped her closed lids, and I leaned down to kiss the trails. Her hands moved up to grip my shoulder blades in a way that broke my heart. She was so scared. I didn't know how to ease that other than to show her, with my body, how much I worshiped her.

I trailed open mouthed kisses down her neck and around to her collarbone, a place I knew she loved. As I continued down between her breasts, I shifted so that I was nestled between her legs. When I moved one hand down to cup one of the beautiful mounds on her chest, her breathing hitched. I kept the slow, sensual pace and brought my mouth down to suck gently on her nipple.

Julie's legs came up to lock behind my back and I felt the heat, as well as the wetness, against my growing erection. She rocked against me, but I wouldn't be hurried. This time, I wanted to take my time and lock it all in my memory. I wanted to remember the way she felt, the way she sighed, the way she smelled. I needed to memorize it for the lonely nights out on the road.

Turning my ministrations to the other breast, I tilted my hips to bring the tip of my dick to her entrance. Her legs unlocked and rested on my hips as she opened wider to accept me into her body. Kissing my way back up, I found her eyes open and filled with unshed tears. I slowly brought my body up, bracing myself with one hand and running the other leisurely down her side to cup her ass cheek and bring her closer. The tip was still the only part of me in her, and while my eyes were locked with hers, I slid in gently.

Bringing my mouth down to hers, I kissed her with the same speed at which I moved in and out, unrushed. Her eyes drifted closed and her hands moved reverently over my back like she too was memorizing my body. She sighed into my mouth, and I took the opportunity to stroke my tongue with hers. A moan traveled through me as she moved her legs to the bed to press up and change the angle. I increased the pressure ever so slightly as well as the speed. Still keeping it steady, I rolled us and brought her so she was straddling me. I held her ass cheeks in both hands to keep her moving slow and I removed my mouth from hers.

She protested for a moment until I lifted and latched on to a nipple. With each tug on her breast, I felt her inner walls clench slightly. She was so close. Her head was thrown back and her hands rested slightly on my abs. Julie was giving up all control to me. I was seeing her as no one else ever would. That thought alone set me off. I started bucking in quick little bursts and she gasped with a slight screech. Letting go of her nipple with a *pop*, I laid back to watch her face. Moving my hands to her hips, I held her down as I continued to pump.

"Evan!" she screamed, just as her inner walls constricted on my dick.

"Julie!" I roared in return as I shot my load into her womb.

I released her hips and moved to sit up, wrapping my arms around her, yet not pulling from her body. She no sooner had come down from her ecstasy when she started sobbing. Her arms came up to loop around my neck while she buried her face in the crook. I held fast, rubbing my hands up and down her back, while I whispered into her ear. Ryan was a stupid fucker, and I'd be damned if he was ever going to get his hands on her again.

"I'm here, baby," I crooned. "I've got you."

JULIE

"ARE YOU READY YET?!" CAME Avery's giggly voice from the bottom of the stairs.

"Hold. On," I grated out, pulling off the shirt I had on and replacing it with another.

Looking around, I let out a *huff*. It looked like a bomb had exploded in my closet. Clothes were strewn about everywhere—shorts, jeans, tank tops, t-shirts. Everything, except my work clothes, was on the floor and covering the bed. I had no idea what to wear.

"Holy shit, woman." Avery laughed as she poked her head in the doorway.

"Ave," I warned, again pulling off the shirt I had on and pulling on a tank top that was flowy and hunter green.

The color worked with my eyes and hair, while the material

was perfect for the muggy weather outside. My hair was pulled half up, and the waves that I had created with the blow dryer seemed to be holding. Tucking my dark skinny jeaned legs into knee-high dark brown boots, I slipped on a couple bracelets and touched my lips quickly with lip gloss. Turning, I looked at myself in the mirror and was satisfied with what I saw.

"Are you nervous, Jules?" she asked, now leaning on the door jamb with a knowing smile on her lips.

I raised an eyebrow at her as I grabbed my purse in an "Are you kidding me?" kind of way, but I couldn't fool her or myself. Of course I was. The guys had been back on tour for almost two months, and I had been going crazy not seeing Evan. It was funny how quickly I had missed his presence despite having pushed him away for so long. We texted and Facetimed as much as we could, yet with his busy schedule and mine, it was difficult.

Tonight, I would finally get to see him. It would only be for a few hours, but it was better than nothing. The guys would be playing just outside of Boston, and we decided to surprise them. Mikey had hooked us up with VIP backstage passes and we would be heading down early to catch the sound check and spend some time with them before the show since their bus would pull out directly after to take them to the airport to head back to Nashville.

Grabbing my overnight bag, I followed her downstairs. I had moved into the other guest bedroom shortly after Dark Roads left. It had made things easier and harder at the same time. Being near Avery, someone who understood what I was going through, made it easier. Being across from his bedroom, and catching whiffs of his cologne every once in a while, made it harder. My apartment was currently empty back in Massachusetts, but I couldn't bring myself to rent it out just yet. My insecurities about my new relationship just wouldn't allow me to.

"How are you not?" I asked her when we had settled into her SUV.

"Not going to lie, I am," she admitted, setting the vehicle in motion, the air conditioner blaring to combat the stickiness of the August afternoon. "However, my excitement of seeing my husband trumps all that."

I could understand that. My nerves couldn't though. I felt like thousands of butterflies had taken up residence in my belly and I couldn't keep my legs from hopping. So that I didn't have a total freak fest, Avery and I started talking about the new office.

The Maine branch of Lane & Son was doing amazing, better than I could have ever asked for. The four new clients I met with just a short time ago had turned into fifteen. It looked like both offices would be about the same size. We had already hired on more people for the new spot and everyone seemed to be the perfect fit. Bringing Ave in as a co-owner had been the best idea we'd had in years. She had really stepped into her role as CEO, and was quickly becoming my go-to when I needed to bounce things off someone. My father was tickled as well. He had told me just the week before that my grandfather would have been proud of me and the path I had taken the company on. It had meant more to me than he knew to hear those words.

"Here we go," Avery muttered, a couple hours later.

We had finally reached the interstate near our exit for the concert venue and the traffic had picked up drastically. It wasn't in Boston, but near enough that getting off was tricky if you weren't used to driving there. Clients of ours were off the same exit, so both of us were used to finagling our way around the area. I closed my eyes, and worked on controlling my breathing and slowing my heart rate. In less than fifteen minutes, we would be there. I would finally get to put my hands on my boyfriend. Wait, boyfriend? That was the first time I had admitted that to myself.

"Shit!" I gasped, opening my eyes.

"What?!" Avery asked pulling off the exit and briefly glancing at me in concern.

"He's my boyfriend," I said.

"Evan?" she questioned, a smile playing on her lips.

"Yeah," I replied, shaking my head. "How did that happen?"

"How could it *not* happen?" She laughed.

"Brat," I returned, smiling myself, leaning over to slap her playfully on the arm.

She was right. How could it not have? The man had chased me to no end, showered me with affection, and had put himself out there all for me. All despite my efforts to put distance between us and keep him at arm's length. Now, I just needed to figure out how I was going to protect my heart if everything went array.

"Stop overthinking," Avery chided, putting her blinker on and turning into the parking lot of a large brick building. "Evan has never given you a reason to question him, so don't start making them up."

Sighing, I reached over and squeezed her hand. She was right. He hadn't. Yet, everything with Ryan was still so fresh and weighed heavy on me. The two were night and day, that I knew, but it still didn't keep the thoughts at bay. While Ryan had broken my heart, Evan had the power to destroy it.

Once we parked and made our way to the side of the building, my nerves turned into excitement. I couldn't wait to be wrapped in his muscled arms and to have those blue eyes locked with mine. I was becoming quickly attached to this man, the one thing I had always prided myself on not doing.

"Well, there are the two most beautiful women in the world," Mikey greeted as we reached one of the main entrance doors.

"You do know we are both spoken for, right?" Avery teased as she stepped into his arms.

"Ah, only you, technically," he chuckled, wrapping his arms around her.

I rolled my eyes, a smile playing on my lips, as he let her go and reached for me. Mikey was Cooper's bodyguard and had been with the band from the beginning. While the others all had individual security as well, he was more like family. Rumor had it he had a younger sister as well, that he didn't see much. Avery had a theory that that was the reason he was always worried and watching out for us. If he couldn't do it for his own blood, then he would do it for the next best thing.

"The guys don't have a clue you're coming," he told us as he led us down a long hallway where the concessions normally would be. "They were just getting on stage when I came to get you. The times got shifted."

When we entered the area where the stage was, I was floored. While I had been to concerts before, it was totally different when all the seats were empty and it was just the band. It was no less awe-inspiring. Their country rock pounded through the space and my heart seemed to beat in time inside my chest. Something was off, though. I couldn't put my finger on it. The music and notes seemed right.

"This way, ladies," Mikey gestured after we had walked down aisles to get us in front of the stage.

A handful of chairs were set up and a few were taken by what looked like reporters or radio personnel. I knew for a fact that the band was pretty strict about who was allowed near them. Problems in the past had led them to tighten security and only deal with people they trusted.

No sooner had we sat down did I realize what was wrong with the music; well, it wasn't the music but rather with Evan. He was playing and from the outside, everything looked fine; however, the smile on his lips as he belted out the lyrics to "Party" with the others didn't reach his eyes. I searched his face and noticed slight smudges under them. *What the hell?*

"Has Cooper said anything to you about Evan?" I asked Avery without taking my eyes from the stage.

"Nope, why?"

"Something isn't right," I told her.

"Haven't you been talking to him?"

"Yeah, but the past week has just been phone calls and text

messages," I replied, finally looking at her. "I was playing catch up at the Mass office, and he was running ragged with concerts."

"He looks okay," she said, turning back to the stage to look at him.

I shook my head. He might have looked like he was fine to the average Joe. I knew better. I'm not sure what bothered me more, that he hadn't talked to me about it or that I hadn't noticed, even through our phone conversations.

Sound check only lasted for about an hour. The guys all seemed really happy with how everything went and didn't want to tire their voices out. As it was, their tour schedule had been a grueling one and still had months to go. Avery and I stood back as they came off the stage, and the others seated next to us approached them. I wasn't even sure they were aware we were there yet, they had been so engrossed in their bubble.

"We're done," I heard Coop's voice tell the group surrounding them, a half hour later. "My woman is here and I need to get my hands on her."

Avery laughed beside me. He was the first one headed our way and only had eyes for his wife. It made my breath hitch the way he looked at her, so full of love from a tattooed hard-ass. Cooper didn't care who was watching. First, he leaned down and whispered to her belly, almost causing me to look away on what should have been a private moment, and then he stood to his full height, cupped her face in his hands, and kissed her like they were alone in their bedroom at home.

"Damn," I heard a voice mutter from beside me. "I have to compete with that."

I turned and found Evan looking at me with a smile, one that again didn't reach his eyes, and noticed that his baby blues were dull and almost lifeless. He pulled me into his arms without hesitation though, and I felt him let out a deep sigh as I wrapped my arms around his neck to pull him closer. He nuzzled into the spot where my shoulder meets my neck and squeezed me so hard I thought I was going to burst.

"Everything okay?" I asked when he finally let up enough that I could lean back and look him in the face.

"Better now that you're here," he told me in a whisper as he leaned down to claim my lips with his.

The kiss was nothing like the others we had shared. It was needy, sad, and desperate. I ran my hands up the back of his neck and into his hair to hold him and changed the angle. I took it deep and showed him with my mouth that I was here for him no matter what. This time, it was my turn to show him that I worshiped him without using any words.

EVAN

I WASN'T SURE IF THE girls surprising us outside of Boston had been good or bad. Having Julie in my arms for a few hours helped ease some of the shit I had been carrying around, but it had also hurt twice as bad to watch her go. Her kisses and quiet murmurs were just what I had needed, but my heart had physically ached at not being able to tell her.

Quietly, I shut the hotel room door behind me and made my way to the elevators. It was three o'clock in the morning and there wasn't a soul in sight. I really should have been in bed, considering we had a show that night; however, sleep just wouldn't come. I had tossed and turned for hours and finally decided I should just make use of the weight room to try and burn off some of my restless energy. I could nap later, after sound check, if I needed to.

When the doors *whooshed* open, I stepped inside and hit the button for the lobby. Before the doors could close, a body slid in and I had to shake my head at my jumpiness. Of course one of the bodyguards was going to follow me. They took rotations at night when we were at hotels, so I didn't know this one's name, but I nodded at him just the same.

Reaching the lobby, I took the left that would take me to the machines first. I figured a warm-up on the treadmill would be a good start and I would move to free weights after. The only people I passed on my way were those who worked at the establishment. The bodyguard was still behind me, I could feel it. Poor guy, he would be bored out of his freaking mind.

"Man, why don't you go get a coffee?" I told him as I opened the door. "I'll be fine, Scout's honor."

"I shouldn't…" he started.

"There isn't anyone around this time of the morning, except the staff," I informed him, gesturing to some of the housekeeping members coming down the hall. "I have my phone if I need anything."

He too looked around. After a few moments of what I could tell was a battle between the devil and angel on his shoulders, the man put his hand out for my phone. I handed it to him and watched as he put his name and number in it. Feeling satisfied I was just fine on my own, he handed it back and turned to head toward the café.

Sighing with relief, I put my earbuds in and walked into the room. It was silent, almost eerily so, since the televisions and radios weren't even on. Cranking up 90's rock on my music app, I jumped onto the nearest machine and got to jogging. My muscles were sore at first, but quickly warmed and the pain became a distant memory.

Most people were surprised that we still worked out when we were on the road; after all, the physical piece of our show should have been enough of a workout. There was no way we could do what we did without putting in both cardio and weights, but it didn't mean I still didn't ache after a good show. Though, I'm sure a good part of it was also that I wasn't eating or sleeping right. Outside stresses after we had gone on tour were taking their toll on my body.

The slowing of the machine alerted me that my time there was done. Getting off, I cleaned it and stretched before walking to the next room. I was alone once again and saw no sign of the bodyguard. Setting myself up for squats first, I got started on the same regimen I did at home. I did a little bit of everything—legs, arms, butt, and back—making sure I hit all the larger muscles.

Metallica pounded into my ears and the sweat started dripping off me. I caught movement out of the corner of my eye, but thought nothing of it. It was pushing four o'clock and I was almost finished my last set of reps. Early birds would be getting up and starting to use the gym or getting breakfast. Putting down my weights after my last set of bicep curls, I saw someone leaning against the wall, watching me.

"What the fuck?" I questioned, shaking my head to make sure I wasn't imagining things.

"You can shake your head all you want, sweetheart"—the woman chuckled—"but I'm not going to disappear, much to your dismay."

Standing on the other side of the room was none other than my mother. Barbara Foster. She looked just like she had eleven years ago when I originally left Maine. Tall, thin, and like she could stand to eat a few donuts. Her blue eyes were dark circles and the lines on her face were more pronounced than they had been years ago. The blonde hair that she had up in a ponytail was bleached and lifeless. I had always wondered if she had a drug problem, but she had never had them around the house, or alcohol either, for that matter.

I didn't know what to say to her or know why the hell she was even here. Growing up, we hadn't been close and by the time I was a teenager, we hardly saw each other. She had made sure our house was clean and there was always food in the refrigerator, but she had almost never been around. I hadn't even said goodbye to her when I packed my bags for Nashville.

When Cooper and I first returned home to Maine last year, I had been surprised to find one of her homemade lasagnas on the deck one night. It included a welcome home note and stupid me started to get my hopes up. That was until she contacted me again only because she wanted more money.

"Why the hell are you here?" I asked, keyed up from the workout and ready for a fight.

"Oh, Evan, is that any way for you to speak to your mother?" she asked, straightening and coming closer to me.

I immediately stepped back and pulled my earbuds out. Shooting a look at the door, I noticed that the bodyguard still wasn't anywhere in sight. So much for thinking I'd be fine on my own. Dumbass.

"Considering you're only that by blood," I murmured, "not by choice, I'd say it's just fine."

The sting of a slap on across my cheek had me wincing. Her eyes filled quickly with hatred, but her mouth moved into a menacing smile. One that had my stomach knotting instantly.

"Now, why did you have to go and say something like that?" she tsked. "I just came to talk to you."

"Then talk," I spit, wiping the sweat from my face with the bottom of my shirt.

"You really need to learn some manners," my mother admonished. "I'm not exactly sure where I went wrong with you. I loved you, and kept you clothed and fed, but are you at all grateful?"

I rolled my eyes and grabbed my water bottle. Looking at my phone, I noticed that I had a text message from Cooper, wanting to know where I was. If he only knew, he would be down here and on her like a dog with a bone. He couldn't stand this woman any more than I could.

"I know what you can do to make up for that," she said, putting her finger to her chin and throwing me another smile that had my gut telling me I wouldn't like what was coming next.

"And what's that?" I asked, trying to figure out how to get her out of here before the other guys in the band came down.

"It seems I have some compromising photos and information that may be bad news for you, your band, and your new lady friend."

I stopped moving and looked up at her. Her grin grew. She knew she had me. I wouldn't do anything to hurt any of them. She was hitting me at my weakest point—those who I felt were my true family.

"If you give me a little spending money, I could make it all go away," came her solution.

I had known that was coming. Shaking my head, I realized I couldn't do this with her anymore. Money really wasn't an issue because I hadn't spent much of what I had earned over the years. Other than helping with the purchase and costs of our Nashville home, everything was invested or in savings.

"You would really do that to your own son?" I asked, not entirely shocked, yet exasperated at the same time.

"The one that isn't appreciative of everything that I did for him growing up? Yes, yes I would."

"Evil bitch," I muttered.

"Funny, your father used to say the same thing," she cackled.

JULIE

I T AMAZED ME HOW QUICKLY I had gotten used to the noise of having the guys in the band around. Not just Evan, but Coop, Matt, and Chris as well. The laughter, testosterone, and smells all brought some level of comfort. Even the arguing was heartwarming; it meant that there was love there.

For the first time I could ever remember, I sat in my office, restless. Usually I thrived on my work and the stress that it could bring; I had been raised on it. More times than I could count, I had come to the office with my father to sit and help him look through numbers. I had been groomed for it.

Looking at the picture of Evan and myself from Avery and Coop's wedding that sat on my desk, I smiled. She had it printed and framed for me when I had started coming to the Maine office. The feelings on both of our faces warmed my heart. If it wasn't love, the friendship alone made me happy. Shifting my gaze, I found the one of my parents and myself. It had been taken at a bank dinner back in Massachusetts, just before I had filled out the paperwork for Avery to become a co-owner. It was the last event my parents would go to as owners of Lane & Son. There was no love there. It looked like three associates, not members of a family.

My phone ringing brought me out of my train of thought. When I looked down, I noticed that Nicole was transferring me a call. It was my father. Speak of the devil.

"Hello, Father," I greeted, leaning back in my chair and kicking off my heels to wiggle my toes.

"Good morning, Juliette," he responded, sounding more like a professional and causing me to cringe when he used my full name.

"Did you receive the email I sent this morning?" I asked, knowing full well he did and had already gone through the information.

"I did," he said. "The numbers are better than expected in the new location."

"They are," I admitted, smiling with pride. "We picked up two more businesses than planned. I also had to hire another accountant."

"Good to hear," he murmured, and I could easily see him looking over the spreadsheets as we spoke.

"I'd like give some of the employees the option to have satellite offices between the two locations."

"Not a bad idea," he agreed. "What about management? Will you and Avery be splitting the offices as originally planned, with you in Massachusetts and her in Maine?"

I felt the blood drain from my face. Pinching the bridge of my nose between my thumb and index finger, I took a deep breath. What I had originally told my father had now changed. Evan had come into the picture and since I wasn't sure exactly what we were, I didn't want to commit to one office. Now, how did I tell *him* that.

"That has not been determined yet," I told him slowly, choosing my words. "I will continue to be at both offices until after Avery has her baby and her husband is back home."

"Understandable. Is she still fully committed to the business?"

"Of course she is," I snapped, sharper than I meant to. "She always has been, otherwise I wouldn't have brought her in."

"I just wanted to check," he argued. "No need to get all emotional."

I got up out of my chair and paced in the little space behind my desk that I could reach with the phone cord. This man was the other one that could get under my skin. All I wanted was the business to officially be mine. It was so close I could taste it.

"I apologize," I managed to get out, even though I really wasn't.

"I'll call Coin and have the paperwork drawn up," he finally said. "The business will officially be yours by the end of the year."

"Thank you," I breathed, doing a little jig.

"Don't thank me," my father replied. "You've earned it. I'm proud of what you have accomplished."

"Thank you," I sputtered.

"You're welcome," he sighed, annoyed with me. "We will talk soon."

With that comment, the call was disconnected. I was so happy, yet sad at the same time. It was a huge relief to know that I would no longer be under my father's hand when it came to the business. It would belong to Avery and myself. I had busted my ass for years to keep the original location up to my father's standards, and we had worked hard to get the new one up and going successfully. It had been a whirlwind since all of this had started just a year prior.

I shouldn't have been sad about anything. My childhood hadn't been filled with hugs, kisses, and affection. It had been much like the business. I had been expected to act a certain way, and I had. There weren't the normal crazy teenage antics or the uncertainty of a major in college. The plan had been for me to take over and I had. There had never been any closeness with my family.

It was probably the reason I had fallen so quickly for Avery and her band of misfits. They had welcomed me with open arms merely because she and I were friends. There was never any question on what I came from or who I was. I had simply been accepted. Evan had just been a bonus.

Though, it didn't mean my heart didn't break a little with the coolness behind my father's voice in the phone call. It didn't matter that I was his little girl. For him, it was all about the business. My parents would be able to travel and retire without a care in the world. Would it even matter to them if I ever got married again or had kids?

Knock! Knock!

"Come in," I said, nearly jumping in my seat at the sound.

"Sorry to interrupt," Avery apologized. "I just wanted you to look at these before I approved them."

"Not a problem," I assured her as I moved around to sit at my conference table and gestured for her to do the same.

She slid the file across the table and I opened it to look at the papers inside. I studied them and didn't find anything out of place. Scrunching up my face in confusion, I closed the file and pushed it back toward her.

"You know those are fine," I stated matter-of-factly. "What's going on?"

"Nicole told me that your father had called, and I wanted to check on you," she admitted, shrugging and giving me a small smile.

I loved this woman. She had become more than a co-worker to me over the years and now I couldn't imagine my life without her. Avery had weaseled her way into my heart, much like Evan. It was nice to have someone be worried about me once in a while.

"He did, and I'm fine," I told her. "Actually, I'm more than fine."

"Oh?" she questioned.

"As of the end of the year, Lane & Son will officially be ours."

"Ours?"

"Yeah, ours." I chuckled at her puzzled expression. "As in, yours and mine."

"Wait, what?"

"My father has approved the final paperwork to be signed, and it will solely belong to the two of us. He will no longer be a shareholder."

"That's so freaking awesome!" she exclaimed. "I can't wait to tell Cooper!"

Rushing from the room, file in hand, I laughed at her. This was exactly why I had pushed for this. She would appreciate the rewards that came after the hard work as much as I did. It wouldn't just be about the money. Avery did have the right idea, though. Other than telling her, Evan was the first one I wanted to tell. Grabbing my phone, I sent him a message.

J: Guess what happened to me today?

EVAN

ONE WEEK. ONE FUCKING WEEK. That was all it had taken for my life to go from being the best it had been to rock bottom. It felt like déjà vu. We had just gone through this with Cooper, only this time, I had someone trying to con money out of me, ruin my new relationship, and get the band some bad publicity. Why the hell couldn't people just let us live our lives and do what we loved?

I had left Maine on a natural high. Julie and I had finally worked things out and were going to try our hands at a long-distance relationship; where she was reserved, I was confident that we could make it work. Avery and Cooper did. She was exactly what I had needed without realizing it. The band had regrouped and recharged, and we were all ready to get back on the road. Even though Coop hated to be away from Avery, we all loved what we did and touring was part of it.

So was this. The stories, the lies, the pictures. All manipulated by the media into what they wanted it to be. I had been pissed when the articles had come out about Cooper that had had Avery questioning their relationship. Now? Now I was beyond that. Anger and frustration over my lack of control of the situation was simmering just below the surface. I wanted to punch something, but knew I couldn't because that would mess things up for the tour and the other guys.

"FUUUUUUUCK!" I roared, swiping my arm across the island in the kitchen and knocking all the magazines to the floor.

"Well, good morning to you too, sunshine," Matt grumbled from the hall, stopping short when he entered the kitchen and saw the mess on the floor.

We had been back in Nashville for a week to perform at a couple spots and get a few tracks done at the studio before we hit the road again. It had been kinda nice to stay in my own bed here rather than in a hotel, though it wasn't as good as it would have been if I had been in Maine. The place I knew I needed to be right now to assure the woman of my dreams I wasn't playing her for a fool. To let her know I was starting to fall in love with her. Instead, I was here and everything was about to fall apart.

"Where the hell did these come from?" he asked as he leaned down to pick them up, and spread them back out on the island.

"I went for a run this morning and when I got back to the gate, the guard had them waiting for me," I said, turning around to grab a water out of the refrigerator, so I didn't have to look at them. "He didn't know the woman that dropped them off."

"Damn," I heard him mutter and then let out a low whistle.

"Yeah, fucking mess," I returned, my voice coming out raspy as I settled in front of the sink, looking out the window.

The emotions were starting to take over. The ones that no one ever got to see. I was a man who believed in crying when the situation called for it. Sometimes you had to. I felt my eyes start to fill and I had to squeeze the bridge of my nose with one hand while the other held me up against the counter. When I opened them, I looked out into the backyard not really seeing much of anything. I didn't want this to bring me down. I didn't want the guys to see the mess I had gotten myself into.

"I think it's time to get the troops together," he told me, just as I heard slight chatter from the direction of the stairs.

"Troops for what?" Cooper questioned, coming into the room with Chris right behind him, both moving toward the coffeemaker.

I didn't turn around. I could hear them behind me and assumed Matt was showing them the magazines. Closing my eyes again, I leaned both arms against the sink.

"Fuck!" Cooper bellowed.

"Shit!" Chris exclaimed.

The tears escaped my eyelids. I couldn't stop them. Now I had to tell them everything; there was no hiding it. I had to man up and face my problems. Unfortunately, doing that meant I was going to lose the one person that meant the most. Her fear would take her from me before I ever got a chance to explain.

Standing up straight, I wiped at my face and was about to turn when I felt Cooper's hand on my shoulder. I knew it was him. We were the closest, and he would always be the first and the last one there for me. When he pulled me in for a man hug, I caught Chris's eye over his shoulder. He gave me a nod as he held his phone to his ear. I knew he was calling Maggie.

As soon as Coop released me, his phone rang, causing my stomach to drop. Immediately, Avery came to mind. He looked at the screen and shook his head. I let out the breath I didn't realize I held and pulled out one of the stools to sit down. He swiped across the screen and greeted someone with a familiar tone before, asking them to hold on and handing me the phone.

"Hello?" I greeted, looking at my bandmate with my eyebrow raised.

"Evan, man, I'm so fucking sorry," Brody's voice filled my ear. "I didn't realize they had gotten in."

Cooper's friend Brody Walker owned the bar we had been at one of the first nights we had been back in Nashville. He had wanted a pair of tickets for our concert, but we had given away our last pair. Instead, we had showed up at Walker's Taphouse the following night to grab supper and hang out with them.

We had a blast. Well, had until some jackass had tried to make off with Brody's girl Lindsey, sending the whole bar into a shit storm. We had cut the music partway through a song to try to help search for the guy, but he had slipped out in the commotion. Security had been scrambling, and somehow the paparazzi had found their way in without us realizing it.

"Brody, it's not your fault," I assured him. "You had your hands full with Lindsey. I would have done the same thing if I had been in your shoes."

"I know, but...fuck..." I could hear him hiss. "This never should have happened. You guys should be able to come here without worrying about that shit."

"It's all part of it," I told him. "We know that. The timing just isn't the greatest."

"If you need anything, hell, if you need me to call that woman of yours, I'll do it. I owe you guys," Brody offered.

"You really don't, man, but I appreciate it just the same," I told him.

We finished with some small talk about Lindsey. I wanted to make sure she was okay. Brody let me know she was definitely shook up, but was handling things as best as could be expected. When the conversation ended, I grabbed the nearest magazine and studied the cover.

The picture was taken as we were leaving the bar. I had my arm wrapped around a woman who was hiding her face in my chest and the guys were flanking me. The sign for the bar was lit behind us and for anyone looking at it, it would seem she had been with me and I was hiding her face to keep it from the tabloids. In reality, it had been Mikey's sister, Kit. She had caught her asshole boyfriend cheating on her and had met us there to unwind since she lived in town. She had been spooked by what had happened and because I was the nice guy, I comforted her. It was in my nature, and I had never even thought twice about it. The title read **Foster Dumps Business Owner for Nashville Flame**.

Tossing that aside, I grabbed another: **Foster Dates Business Owner to Help Pay Back Debt**. The article in that one was a hoot. All about my supposed gambling problem and that I needed Julie to support my habit. The picture was one of us in Maine outside The Full Belly. She was looking up at me and I had my hands on her cheeks. I wasn't even sure who had taken it.

Shoving that one over, I looked at the one under it: **Mother Comes Forward about Dark Roads' Guitarist's Gambling Problem**. That one had me seething, especially since there was a picture from my childhood on it with my mother and myself. That woman had nothing to do with my career, yet had suddenly felt like it was time to let everyone know she was the one who had given birth to me. To think I had tried so hard to keep her quiet.

The last one made me want to hop on a plane and head to Maine immediately. It was also the most confusing, as it told a different story from the others. The picture was one of Julie and Ryan from some function, and the title read **Maine Business Woman uses Dark Roads' Foster to Make Husband Jealous**. The article was about how Julie was only dating me to get to her soon-to-be ex, as well as needing my money to keep her business afloat. All of it was bullshit. It was one thing for them to write about us, but to throw her in the mix was unacceptable.

"Maggie will get this all taken care of," Coop said confidently as he set a mug down in front of me.

We could still hear Chris on the phone, with who I was now assuming was Lee, our manager and his uncle. It didn't sound like a good conversation. Matt patted me on the back and started rummaging around in cupboards. While I nursed my cup, he set out making pancakes. If there was one thing we could all do, stress or not, it was eat. Cooper got up to help.

"I'm sorry, man," Chris apologized when he sat down next to me moments later.

"For what?" I asked, looking up from my coffee.

"I tried to get Lee to change the tour a bit so you could go back to Maine, but we are too tight."

"I appreciate that, but we have to get back on the road." I put my hand on his shoulder. "I get that. I will deal with things there the best I can from here."

"This shouldn't be happening," he mumbled. "Not to you."

"Someone had better have food ready for me if you are going to call me this early," came Maggie's booming voice before I could ask Chris what he meant.

"I got ya covered, darlin'," Matt let her know as she stepped into the room.

She grinned at him, her red hair and green eyes sparkling as she made her way over to kiss me on the cheek before getting herself some coffee. Maggie may have looked like a petite, sweet woman, but we knew better. She was a spitfire who fought tooth and nail for what she believed in. We counted our blessings every day that she had stuck with the band. She jokingly told us on a regular basis that we kept her plenty busy so she didn't need a standard nine-to-five desk job, and that her other clients got jealous of us.

Fifteen minutes later, we were all sitting around the island, elbow to elbow, eating pancakes with bacon and sipping on our coffee. I think we needed the comfort of each other's presence, or at least I did, so we opted to stay there rather than move to the dining room with the larger table. The only person we were missing was Lexie who, thank God, was in Maine. I had one glimmer of hope that she could keep Julie from leaving me.

"Okay, so, what the hell stirred up this hornet's nest?" Maggie asked, chewing thoughtfully.

"I did," I admitted, putting down my cup and looking up at all of them. "I paid my mother fifty thousand, back when we first started, to back off and leave me alone."

"Without coming to me?" she huffed as the eyes of my band-mates grew large.

"It was before you were with us," I reminded her. "When I say early on, I mean *early on*. Like, I had to take out a personal loan to pay it."

"That's a whole other conversation, but we will address that later. It still doesn't answer the question of what is dragging all this crap up."

"Yeah it does," I replied, my voice going quiet. "She has been calling me asking for more money and threatening me. I sent her another ten thousand, and hoped it would shut her up."

"Oh, darling," she crooned.

I was afraid to break eye contact with her. The guys were quiet and all of them had stopped eating. I could only imagine what was going through their heads. I had brought all this on the band. I was a worthless piece of shit; well, I felt like one.

"What a bitch," Cooper muttered.

"How the hell does she feel that you owe her anything?" Matt spit.

"How do we clear all this up, Mags?" Chris asked.

"Oh, we will, and we will get some payback of our own," she said, leaning over to cover my hand with hers. "That witch won't know what hit her."

JULIE

DUDO...DUDO...DUDO.

My phone wouldn't stop. I wanted to just turn it off; if it hadn't been for the business, I would have. Seeing it was another call from Avery, I swiped to ignore it. Turning, I tried to focus back on the paperwork on my desk.

"Okay...Where the hell is it?" I mumbled to myself.

The numbers started to blur. I pinched the bridge of my nose and closed my eyes on a sigh. My balance sheet didn't balance. How the hell did that happen? Oh, because I couldn't concentrate enough to make sure that everything was assigned to the lines they were supposed to be.

"Ugh!" I groaned, putting my head down on my desk with a *thud*.

"Can I get you anything before I go?" I heard Kelly ask from my doorway.

"A new brain would be wonderful," I muttered not moving my head.

"Honey, why don't you just go home and get some rest."

I waved her out and heard her chuckle as her heels clicked down the hallway. Picking up my head, I stretched my neck and rubbed my eyes. It was after five, and there really was no need for me to stay. My work was caught up here and Avery had the Maine location running like a dream.

Dudo...dudo...dudo.

Evan. That's right, that's why I was staying. Swiping across the screen, I flipped my phone over and got back to the inconsistency on my screen. I didn't want to think about him, or what could have been. I had been played and it wouldn't happen again.

Two hours later, my eyes couldn't take anymore. I turned off my computer, packed up a couple files, and made my way out of the office. After making sure everything was locked up I made the short drive to my duplex. When I turned off my car, I sat for a moment. My heart was heavy.

For so long, this place had been home. I had been proud to buy it on my own and fix it up. Now, it just felt like the walls were closing in when I was there. It wasn't the place I truly wanted to be. I wanted to be back in Maine, but it hurt too bad to be there.

Grabbing my bags, I got out and headed for the house. Kelly's lights were on and there was a truck I didn't recognize in the driveway. Male laughter wafted through the cracked window and tears pricked my eyes when hers answered back. I pushed open the door and when I clicked on the light, I froze.

The spread of magazines across my countertop drew my gaze immediately. It was like a damn car crash that you can't look away from. Lexie had tried to soften the blow, but there was nothing she could say or do that would make me feel better about what he had done. Pictures spoke a thousand words. I had set

THE UNKNOWN | 101

eyes on them, packed my stuff up, and moved back to Massachusetts.

I didn't need Avery or Lexie to give me excuses. They would always stand up for him, even if he had done something wrong. I had known opening my heart to him would kill me, eventually, and slowly it was. The only thing I could promise myself was that I wouldn't let my clients suffer for it. I would reach out to Avery with regard to work, but I would shoot her down the minute she brought up anything about him. For a little while anyway, she was just my partner in Lane & Son.

Locking the door behind me, I emptied my hands and made my way to the refrigerator. Given how late it was, I decided on a yogurt and a banana. I wasn't overly hungry anyway. As I took a spoonful of the strawberry mixture, I let my eyes be drawn to the cover with Evan and another woman on it. According to the article and my friends, it was Mikey's sister, Kit. I had heard very little about her, and I guess I knew why now. My stomach threatened to revolt with the thought and I had to take a couple of deep breaths to finish the carton.

Now the night at the concert made total sense. He had been eaten alive with guilt. Hiding his relationship with her must have been hard on him given how often we had been talking. It was quite a feat for him to juggle two of us, on top of the touring schedule Dark Roads had been on. Well, he didn't have that problem anymore, did he?

Snickering, without humor, I slid that one to the side and found the one about us. At least that one I knew wasn't true. Evan had never in any way wanted my money for anything, and he sure as hell didn't have a gambling problem. I wasn't sure where that was coming from, which made the one about his mother just as confusing. Last I knew, he hadn't had any sort of contact with her. She had basically ditched him as a child, only supporting him enough so that the state didn't come after her.

And then there was the one about me. That one just made my

blood boil. The only people who knew the things in that article were Evan and Ryan. I knew it couldn't have been my ex because the articles were written by idiotic professionals that couldn't have cared less about him. I just couldn't believe that Evan had stooped that low. I had thought so much more of him. He had the good-guy routine down pact. Ass.

Shaking my head, I threw my container away. It was over and done with now. I should have known better. Hitting the lights, I headed to my bedroom. Sleep would be hard coming, but I couldn't do any more work. My brain was mush.

Stripping off my clothes in the dark, I climbed between the sheets. The windows were open a crack, and I could faintly hear Kelly and her companion. Tears welled up in my eyes as I got comfortable. The cotton against my skin just reminded me of that first morning with Evan. How good it had felt in his bed. The feelings I had known were already starting even then.

Soon, there were trails streaming down my face. My heart was heavy in my chest. My eyelids fluttered closed and I snapped them open again. Evan's face would show up every time. His smile, those eyes, the dimples. I had thought he was perfect. I couldn't believe I had been so wrong. That's probably what bothered me the most.

The next morning, I was up with the sun. Dragging my exhausted body out of bed, I pulled on clothes to go running. After putting my hair into a messy bun, I slid my cell phone into my armband. It had become my routine to get a run in before work. Tiring my body out before and my brain during the day was the only way I could think of to keep the depression that was threatening to pull me under, at bay.

Switching the station to 90's pop, I finished tying my laces and stretched lightly. When I made my way out the door and started down the driveway, I heard a noise behind me. Turning my head slightly, I saw Kelly walking out her friend from the night before. He was a good-looking, clean-cut guy. Before I could see the farewell exchange, I popped my earbuds in and turned down the road. I was happy for her, but I didn't need any reminders of what I was missing out on.

A few hours later, I was unlocking the door and making my way into the office. I'd have it all to myself for about twenty minutes before Kelly would be in with our iced coffees. This was the best part of the day. This was the only time I felt just a little bit like the woman I knew I was, capable and confident.

Like clockwork, an iced coffee appeared on my desk, along with a raspberry scone from the nearby bakery. No words were exchanged, as I was on a conference call with a client that needed their feathers fluffed, but I smiled as she set them down. I had known the day was going to be a crazy one the minute I opened my email and found five from said client, all written before six o'clock that morning.

It seemed that the board was looking to switch to a different management company because, quote "we weren't doing enough," and the onsite manager, as well as the president of the board, were fighting it. I spent the better part of the morning pacing my office as I had them on speakerphone, assuring them I would put a proposal together that included all we had done for the company. I had just hung up, pulled off my shoes, and was wiggling my toes to release some tension when my door opened, and I could hear Kelly telling someone they couldn't just walk in.

"I'm still married to her, I can do what I damn well please," Ryan informed her as he walked in ahead of her.

"It's fine, Kelly," I told her as she glared heatedly at his back.

Turning on her heel, she closed the door behind her with a huff. I rolled my shoulders back and slipped into my heels so I was at least a little closer to my ex's six-one height. Ryan was a good-looking man, I would give him that. Standing in front of me with a charming smile, perfectly-styled blond hair, and his five-hundred-dollar suit, he was the epitome of the successful businessman. He was also the man all the women in the office wondered what it would be like to be with. *He's not worth it, ladies*, I thought to myself.

"What can I do for you, Ryan?" I asked, coming around my desk to lean on it, crossing my feet at the ankles and my arms across my chest.

I was actually surprised I hadn't heard from him before now. I had met with my lawyer the previous week and we had done another workaround to Ryan's demands on our divorce. He was fighting to get something from the company, but I had protected that with iron when we married. There was no way I had been willing put what my family worked so hard for on the line. Much to my dismay, my lawyer had suggested just giving him some money so he would hopefully slink away, with a clause that said he couldn't come sniffing for more. Not that he needed it either way.

"I got some paperwork and wanted to talk to you about it," he said, raising his hand with a manila envelope in it.

"I think we are done talking," I retorted. "You can call Coin with any questions."

He closed the distance between us and I fought to keep myself from moving. I didn't want to give him the satisfaction of knowing I didn't want him in my space. Ryan stopped just before our feet touched and brought his hand up to run it along my jawline. I jerked my head and my body tensed beneath his touch. A chuckle escaped him as he cupped my chin in his hand to keep my face still.

Moving my hands, I placed them on my desk and gripped the edge. I was too damn stubborn to pull away. God forbid he tried to kiss me; he would get what was coming to him. Our eyes locked and I could see the sparkle in his. He was going to try to kiss me. Ass.

"You know," he murmured, widening his stance and leaning in. "We were so good together. We could just forget this little shit show ever happened."

Before I could respond, I heard the door open behind him and again, Kelly was in the process of saying, "You can't go in there."

"Get. Your. Fucking. Hands. Off. My. Woman."

EVAN

W HEN THE MAN BLOCKING JULIE from my view didn't move, I stopped and balled my hands into fists. I would not give anyone another reason to plaster us all over the front of a tabloid. The temper I was barely keeping in check turned my body hot. I saw his back tense under his suit jacket, but he gave no other outward sign of hearing me or of moving away from her.

"I said. Get. Your. Fucking. Hands. Off. My. Woman," I repeated through clenched teeth.

Ryan finally stood to his full height, straightened his jacket, and turned. Granted, I had lost a little weight with the stress of everything, but I hadn't stopped lifting. I had muscles that he didn't, and the t-shirt and jeans I wore didn't hide them. I saw him try to fight the fear that he was no match physically with his cool sophistication. The corner of my mouth quirked despite my anger.

"Technically, she's still mine, Foster," he reminded me, a grin of his own filling his face.

I ignored his shot, turning my attention to Julie to quickly assess whether she was all right. She had stood as soon as her ex was out of her space, and slid quietly away, back behind her desk, her fingers touching the top as she watched us. Her eyes had dark smudges under them and it looked like she, too, had lost weight. The tight lipped face she had let me know she was pissed—at both of us, I assumed—yet the glint in her eye told me she was happy I had interrupted.

"Maybe on paper, Cobourne," I replied, letting a Cheshire smile out, "but her body is mine."

I heard Julie gasp, and knew I would have to apologize for that later, but the blanching of Ryan's face made it all worth it. I could see him trying to come up with a response. Seconds passed before an almost evil smile replaced the nauseated look that had come from my comment. Buttoning his jacket, he turned to Julie.

"We're not done talking, lovey," he crooned smoothly and quietly, causing Julie to cross her arms once again and lift her chin. "I'll be in touch. You'll find that I am the much better man for you."

He turned back and moved toward me. I took a deep breath and made sure my arms remained at my sides. He stopped when we were shoulder to shoulder, him facing the door and me still facing Julie. My eyes locked with hers as he started to speak in a low voice, one I was pretty sure was meant for my ears only.

"Those articles were just the beginning, Foster. You won't win this."

Before I could say anything, he continued on his way out the still open door. Knowing Julie would kick me out the quickest she could, I turned away from her and closed the door after shooting Kelly a quick nod. I could see her heading this way, and I needed to speak my piece before she interrupted. I took another deep breath and turned back once I heard the soft *click* of the striker engaging.

"Evan, I think...." she started, the minute our eyes connected again.

"You don't get to think right now," I told her, moving so that I mirrored her stance from in front of the desk, arms crossed and feet braced. "You get to listen."

"You've been ignoring me and I get that, but you don't get to ignore Lex and Avery," I continued. "They have been your friends, your sisters, and you don't get to drop them like bad habits."

"That's none of your business."

"Bullshit, it isn't!" I roared, startling us both. "I have both of them calling me, near tears, because you've withdrawn into yourself and they are worried about you."

I saw her look of shock and moments later watched as she deflated completely. Pulling her arms from her closed-off stance, she put them on her desk to steady herself as she dropped her head. Her back heaved with deep slow breaths and I hoped like hell she didn't cry. I couldn't take that. I was doing all I could as it was not to reach out and touch her.

"I'm worried about you, boss lady," I whispered, again mirroring her and bringing my head close to hers over the desk.

That did it. I saw the first tear splash on the wood and I cursed. *Fuck. Fuck. Fuck.* I moved, not even realizing what I was doing until I was around the desk. I pulled her up and into my arms, holding her tight when she pounded on my chest with her fists and sobbed, swearing and cursing at me between them. I held strong, apologizing in low, soothing tones. Finally, she gave up her fight and sank into me, shaking as she released her tirade of emotions.

I'm not sure how long I held her that way. Finally, her sobs turned to sniffles. I picked her up and moved us to the couch, moving papers with one hand as I held her in the other. When we settled, I wrapped one arm around her and used the other to wipe away the stray hairs that were sticking to the tear tracks on her face. She wouldn't bring her eyes up to meet mine. Putting my fingers beneath her chin, I tilted her head up and they did, albeit reluctantly. There was still anger flashing in them and I knew this fight was just getting started.

"We have other things to discuss. I am going to give you two options. You can either finish the day here and I will wait for you, or you can pack a bag and we will go back to your house now."

"You are not my father, Evan Foster," she snapped, her eyes starting to clear and her body stiffening in my arms.

"I'm fully aware," I said dryly. "But I'm limited on time and we are going to get this sorted out before I go."

"I'm not going to fall back into bed with you," she muttered, looking down to fiddle with her bracelets.

"I didn't expect you to," I replied softly, sadly. "Though it will happen again, I promise you that."

My semi-teasing tone brought out a small smile, but she quickly cleared her face and moved to get up. I released her. I would never force anything on her; however, we needed to talk. If I could at least fix things between her and the girls, I would feel ten times better. She went to her desk, the professional side of her back in place. While she wiped her eyes with a tissue, she shut down her computer and buzzed Kelly to come in.

I sat quietly, letting her gather her things. When the receptionist stepped in, she looked at me with curiosity and mild concern. Julie let her know that she would be leaving early and to only forward a call if it was an emergency. Her friend nodded and shot me another look. She whispered something to Julie I couldn't hear, but only received a slight shake of the head in response. Leaving us alone again, Kelly went back out front. I moved to stand by the door to wait for her and when she approached me with two bags—one with files and one with her computer—I reached for them.

The fight was in her eyes; I could see it when her brown ones met my blue ones. I shook my head with a smile and took them from her anyway. She moved by me and I put my hand on the small of her back. Again, she stiffened. Those articles had certainly done their damage. Julie was right back where she had been when we had first met; walls up and heart guarded.

I followed her back to her duplex and when I parked behind her, I could see her eyes watching me in her mirrors. If she thought I'd been kidding, she was in for a rude awakening. I would get a chance to tell my side of the story. Once I was done, she could decide what she wanted to believe.

Turning off my truck, I climbed out and started toward her car. Before I could open the door, she did it herself and stepped out, reaching back in to grab her bags. I took them from her without a word and gestured toward the house. With a light *huff* that had me smiling, I walked behind her to the door. When she opened it and walked in, I stepped up behind her and set the bags down in the entryway. The magazines on the counter caught my attention immediately, and I saw her face pale when she realized I had seen them.

She moved quickly to dispose of the things before I could get to them, but I covered ground quicker than she did and put my hands over hers so she couldn't. I hadn't realized the position I had put us in and had to take a deep breath to calm my body, as my front was directly against her back with my arms trapping her. Steeled in front of me, Julie froze. My dick automatically went from half-staff to fully hard just being near her, never mind her vanilla smell that filled my nostrils.

Figuring I would use this to my advantage, I shifted our hands so that the magazines were in a pile. The one on top was the one with the picture of Kit and myself. I heard her sigh haggardly and knew she had closed her eyes.

"Open them," I instructed sharply, putting my mouth to her ear. "Look at it."

She shuddered, but I saw her do so.

"That was taken after Brody, the owner of the bar, had someone try to kidnap his woman. Kit had come to see Mikey and hang out with us because she had just busted her boyfriend and her best friend in bed together. We were all watching out for her. The attempt had rattled her, so we all walked out together and went back to the house. She stayed with Mikey that night, as far as I know."

I felt her let out a breath, yet stiffen further against my body.

"Nothing. Happened. Between. Us," I told her, clearly enunciating each word and feeling her flinch with each hard syllable.

Moving them again, the one about my dating her for her money was now on top.

"I'm pretty sure I don't need to explain this one. You know I sure as hell don't want you for your money," I spat.

Another flip had the one about my mother now showing. This time, it was me that tensed.

"I'm not sure where the hell this one came from. Maggie is doing some digging, along with our publicist. Okay, that's a lie. I do know, but it's part of a longer story. I gave her money when we first signed, using a personal loan, and small amounts again when she started calling after we went back on tour in June. I figured it would be enough to shut her up and get her out of my life. Evidently, that didn't work," I ended with a mutter of frustration.

"You never said…"

"I never told anyone," I bit out. "It wasn't anyone's business."

Finally, I came to the one about her using me to make Ryan jealous. The one I had a feeling came from her ex after the comment he had just made to me.

"I know this one isn't true, and I'm pretty sure this all came from Ryan himself…"

I didn't get a chance to finish that sentence because I had an elbow to the gut that surprised me enough I stepped back and put my hand over it. Julie turned, again crossing her arms over her chest, and the pissed off look was back in full force. I put my hands up in surrender and stepped back a little bit more. What the hell?

"You expect me to believe that some reporter searched him out for that information?" she asked hotly.

"Either that, or he went to them, because when he left your office today, he informed me that those articles were just the beginning and that I wouldn't end up with you."

She grew quiet, I could see the wheels turning. Her eyes closed and, seconds later, popped back open. A curse followed. This time, I had a feeling the anger wasn't geared at me, but rather at her ex.

"I guess that means I need to do some digging of my own," she mumbled, uncrossing her arms before letting them dangle at her sides, a ghost of a smile coming to her lips. "Oh, and Evan, I'm still not yours."

JULIE

"You've got to be fucking kidding me," I muttered as I set my coffee down a little too hard, causing the top to pop off the cheap plastic travel cup. "Shit!"

"You having a tough one already?" Avery asked with a chuckle as she entered the kitchen. "It's only seven o'clock and you're already swearing like a sailor."

Shaking my head as I reached for a napkin to clean up my mess, I motioned to the magazine on the table. I had been up since five, had a run, checked in on Evan's house, showered, and stopped by the local chain coffee shop. My nerves of being back in Maine had kept me from sleeping, and when I saw the magazine on the doorstep when I returned, I had gone from uneasy to pissed.

"What the hell?" she mumbled, absently rubbing her very pregnant belly while she read the article.

"Evan didn't do that," I told her defiantly while I put the cover back on my coffee.

"Honey, I know that," she soothed, looking at me with understanding in her eyes.

"Sorry, I know you do," I apologized. "I just don't understand what Ryan thinks he stands to get out of all this."

"You," she says simply. "He wants you back."

"For what?!" I questioned, standing back up to pace. "He didn't want me when he was banging his secretary."

"Have you heard from Evan, Maggie, or Tracey?" she asked. "Did they find anything?"

"Not yet." I shook my head, stopping to sip my fuel. "I think it's time to make some phone calls."

"Well, let's get going then," she agreed, getting up and heading back toward her bedroom to get ready to go to the office.

Watching her, I smiled. Evan and I still had a lot to work out, but Avery had welcomed me back with open arms. She didn't question why I had put the distance between us, just teared up when she opened the door for me, and hugged me as best her belly would allow. Ave knew my history, knew me, and got me better than anyone else in my life. Probably because she was the only one I let in, other than Evan. Lexie, on the other hand, had gone up one side of me and down the other before she had hugged me and called it good. I was one lucky woman to have the two of them.

Less than a half hour later, we were headed for our Maine office. It felt good to be back. With my friend and co-owner nearing her due date, I was needed here to make sure the new office was running smoothly and that Avery was taken care of. Her pregnancy was going fantastically, but the fact that Cooper was gone was definitely taking its toll.

"Are you all set to handle the meeting with Stilpen?" I asked, as we pulled to a stop in the parking lot and I turned off my car.

"Yep, it's just a check-in to make sure that they are happy with how things are going, and to answer any questions," she reminded me. "They are still nervous about having swapped to us after being with their original management company for ten years."

"I know how that is," I said, climbing out and then reaching into the back for my bags. "If you need anything, just buzz me. I'm going to make a couple personal calls before my lunch meeting with Jennifer."

"Will do, boss lady," Avery retorted with a grin.

I rolled my eyes at her and held the door open for her. I couldn't contain the smile that escaped at the name. Evan hadn't made a secret of calling me that in front of everyone, and each time he did, a tingle would run through me. I wasn't ready to hand my heart back to him just yet though.

Making my way past the receptionist, I sent her a wave since she was on the phone and headed to my office. While she wasn't Kelly, Nicole was very capable and was a quick learner. I was crossing my fingers and toes between her and the new staff we would be okay with Avery out on maternity leave.

Putting my bags down by the small conference table, I closed my door, signaling I was not to be disturbed. I pulled my computer out, setting it on my desk, and plugged it in while it booted up. I was going to need the battery power today. Reaching for my cell phone, I nearly jumped out of my skin when there was a quiet knock on the door. It opened and Lexie poked her head around it. I waved her in.

"I take it you already saw it?" she questioned, putting her briefcase on the table and setting down a copy of the magazine I had seen this morning.

"It was on the doorstep when I got back from grabbing coffee," I told her as I scrolled through the numbers in my contact list. "He didn't do it."

"Jules, you don't need to tell me that," she assured.

I rubbed my forehead and smiled sheepishly at her. I knew I

didn't need to defend him to the people that knew him, but it was a knee-jerk reaction. The negative media attention was making me mad. Finding the number I was looking for, I hit send and motioned for her to sit.

In black dress slacks and a three-quarter cut length olive green shirt that brought out her skin tone beautifully, she lowered herself into one of the comfortable leather chairs in front of my desk while I paced behind it. While Lexie didn't work, per se, she kept herself busy doing odd jobs. Whether it be helping Maggie with stuff for the band or helping me in the office, she was turning out to be quite the asset.

"Eric," I greeted. "How are you?"

My professional yet business tone told the man on the other end that this wasn't a social call. I needed answers, and I was going to get them. Eric Witherall worked under the umbrella company that my ex did, Dawson & Associates. They didn't work in the same office, but the company wasn't so big that he didn't know him. Eric and I had clicked from day one of meeting, and often worked together when I had been in Massachusetts. His office was in New York; however, he often traveled to Boston for meetings. He was an amazing financial analyst, twice the one that Ryan was.

"Good to hear," I told him when he told me he had met a new woman and was happy for the first time in a long time. "I was wondering if you could do some research for me?"

Fifteen minutes later, I was off the phone and Lex and I were sitting at the table, her computer between us. Maggie had sent over some financials she had found and I was going through them with a fine-tooth comb. They belonged to Colbourne Enterprises. It was company owned by my ex-father-in-law, yet was run solely by Ryan when he wasn't working for Dawson. Something about the whole thing just didn't seem right. The magazine at my elbow caught my attention again, pulling me away from the numbers. I sighed when I took it in.

There was a picture on the cover of Ryan, clad with a black eye, swollen almost shut, and a fat lip. He looked like he had taken quite the beating. The title made my temper flare: **Dark Roads' Foster Sends Message to Girlfriend's Ex**. Inside was an article about how Evan had confronted him at my office, and that once the two were alone in the parking lot, he had beat Ryan up without just cause. Even though I knew none of that had happened, as did those who knew Evan personally, the damage to Dark Roads career could be detrimental.

I knew, without a doubt now, that Ryan was fueling this fire, and I would get to the bottom of it one way or another. Focusing back on the numbers, I suddenly saw something that jumped out at me. Actually, two somethings. Those descriptions didn't quite fit the type of business this was supposed to be.

"Are you ladies going to Willie's tonight for the Halloween party?" I heard Lex asked, my brain barely registering what she said as it hummed with information.

"Yep," I replied, short and curt. "Where is the detail to these accounts?"

"Umm…" I saw her out of the corner of my eye going through files. "Right here."

She handed it to me with a questioning look. I grabbed it, nearly dropping it in my haste to see it. Feeling a hand on my arm, I looked up. Lexie smiled and moved her free hand to signal that I needed to slow down. I took a deep breath and opened the file. Flipping through the hundreds of pages, I finally found one of the accounts I was looking for. Revenue. Money coming from the unknown parent company of the magazine releasing the articles. *Bingo*. Pulling those aside to give to Lex, I kept going. Expenses. Money paid to Barbara Smith, large chunks, all just before the articles came out. A common name. Who was she?

"Who is Barbara Smith?" I asked, bringing my eyes up to meet my friend's.

"I'm not sure," she said, her brow furrowing in confusion.

I turned the paper her way and pointed my finger at the numbers. Her eyes grew large and her mouth opened in a perfect O. Her fingers quickly moved to her phone and I heard the tell-tale ringing, signaling a FaceTime session with someone. Maggie answered with a professional hello.

"Hey, Mags, I'm with Julie, and she came across something," she told her, turning the phone slightly so that her wife could see both of us.

"What's that?" Maggie asked, moving so that she could put her phone down and have her hands ready to type on her computer if she needed to.

"Who is Barbara Smith?" I questioned.

Her face showed a look of confusion at first. I saw her type something slowly. Eventually, her fingers were clicking away at a high speed and a grin was growing on her face. Lexie and I exchanged looks, her shoulders going up in a shrug. I looked back at the screen. Maggie was moving her mouse around and seemed to find what she was looking for. An *ah-ha* expression came over her face before she moved the computer so we could see what she found.

"Barbara Smith aka Barbara Foster is Evan's mother," she said with glee.

"Yes!" we cheered, me and Lexie's hands meeting in a high five.

The dots were all being connected and everything was coming together. Just as my friend got up to scan the documents back to Maggie, so she could do her part with them, my phone rang. When I saw it was Eric, my heart started to race.

"Hello," I greeted, getting up to stretch my legs and work off some of the adrenaline coursing through me. "You did? He does?"

The smile on my face grew as his voice filled my ear with the knowledge of what he had uncovered. I was dancing on my toes by the time Lexie returned from the scanner, and she gripped my hands without knowing what I was so happy about. Squeezing hers, I tried to focus on what Eric was saying.

"No wonder he has been fighting the divorce," I murmured, sobering a bit. "That's exactly what I needed to know. I can't thank you enough, Eric. Can you send that information over as soon as possible?"

EVAN

T HE PLANE RIDE SEEMED TO take forever. It was almost two in the morning when I stumbled up the steps of my new house in Maine, fumbling with the lock. I couldn't even appreciate how far it had come since the last time I had seen it. Rubbing my eyes and using my phone as a flashlight, I made my way to rear of the house and the master bedroom. The house was cool since it was late October, and the heat was only on enough to keep things from freezing. I just about tripped over some tools left out in the hallway and cursed when my elbow connected with the beam in the wall rather than a finished product.

I had asked the contractor to make sure the kitchen, my bedroom, and a bathroom were done first, in case I came home before it was complete. I didn't want to have to stay with Cooper and Avery any longer since they were almost ready to welcome a new baby into their lives. I reached my destination and let out a sigh. The door was shut and not thinking anything of it, I opened it, almost letting it bang with my haste. That's when I saw the outline of someone curled under the blankets on my bed. The edge of the light beam from my flashlight didn't tell me who it was, but I knew. Her smell told me.

My cock rose to attention. We hadn't talked much in the last month since I had been home last, but her sleeping in my bed had to be a good sign. She and Avery hadn't known that Coop and I were coming home. The other man had been itching to see his very pregnant wife, so I had offered to come with him. It would only be for a couple of days, but it was better than nothing.

Setting my bags down, I quietly did a scan of the room, keeping my light down so I didn't wake her. The new furniture had been brought in and was exactly where I would have put it. My bed was in the center and was placed so that it faced the French doors that led out to what would be the wrap around porch, the bureau was on the left and shared a wall with the master bath, and my TV had been mounted in the corner on the back wall as well. Moving slightly, I noticed my recliner was on the other side of the bed, along with the second bureau and an armoire. Julie didn't know it yet, but those pieces were for her.

Not wanting to crawl into bed smelling like I did, I made my way to the bathroom with my bag in my hand. I shut the door behind me before reaching for the switch. It was set on a dimmer, so I turned it up only part way. The two sinks were on the left and between them was a small window that looked into the backyard. A shower large enough for two was on the right, along with a toilet and a corner tub. A small shelving system, that was already filled with towels and toiletries, was in the opposite corner. She had thought of everything.

Putting my bag down, I turned on the water in the shower and put it on as hot as I could handle. Stripping out of my clothes in one motion, I grabbed a towel from the shelf and hung it on the hook before climbing in. The glass steamed up immediately. Bracing my hands on the wall under the stream, I closed my eyes and hung my head to let the water cascade over my tired body.

My muscles slowly started to relax, all except my dick that couldn't stop thinking about Julie's soft, warm body that was in my bed waiting. I took one hand from the wall and gripped myself gently, moving my hand up and down in slow strokes. I couldn't climb into bed this hard or I would never get to sleep. Running my finger over the tip, I used the precum and the water flowing down my body as lubrication to continue. Picturing my woman's face behind my closed lids, I pretended my hand was hers. My need for her was so strong I could smell the vanilla stronger than I could before and I swore her smaller hands were smoothing over my hips and covering my larger one on my straining erection. I imagined her wet breasts pressed against my back and her nest brushing against my backside as she melded her body to mine.

"Boss lady," I groaned on a whisper.

"Handsome," I heard her return.

Snapping my eyes open, I looked down. I hadn't been dreaming. Her small, delicate, yet capable, hands were wrapped around my cock and her nails every so often would catch the skin lightly, causing me to twitch. I took my hand off the wall and reached around to grip her ass and pull her leg up to wrap around my hip. The motion caused her hands to move to my sides to keep from falling, but I didn't care. I needed to feel her. Her wetness met my back, and I leaned my head against her shoulder with a low groan. I was so hard, it fucking hurt. I wanted her.

Julie ran her hands up from my lower stomach to my belly button and across each plain of my abs. She rocked against my back and took the opportunity to kiss and nip along my neck while I still rested against her. A slight purr in my ear was my undoing. I dropped her leg and spun around to pin her against the wall, our eyes meeting for the first time.

"I need to be inside you," I growled, my dick pushing against her belly.

"So what are you waiting for?" she asked with a sultry smile, her arms circling my neck and her leg again coming up to wrap around to my ass.

"Are you sure?" I asked in a strained voice as I ran one hand from her ass cheek up her thigh, and bucked my hips against her.

"Yes," she breathed, closing her eyes.

Moving my other hand to her other leg, she hopped, and I picked her up. Julie's feet immediately dug into my lower back and I quickly lined up with her center before I shoved into her hard. I felt myself pulse the minute I was inside, and I had to still to keep from coming like a high schooler. I rested my forehead against hers and heard her whimper.

"It's going to be over before it begins if you don't stop moving," I warned with a hiss.

"Please," she pleaded.

I opened my eyes again and found her looking at me with unshed tears. The emotions rolling in her eyes had my heart breaking. This woman was going to be the death of me. I needed her like I needed air. She completed me and damn, if three little words weren't on the tip of my tongue to say to her, with the look she was giving me. I refused to do it during sex though, and instead brought my mouth down to give her the sweetest and gentlest kiss I could. My mouth showed her the love I couldn't yet confess.

With her tongue circling mine slowly, lazily, and her hands buried in my hair, I shifted and started to rock her gently up and down on my shaft. Our languid movements didn't take away from the intensity of the moment. Our eyes remained open, watching each other and taking everything in. When I felt her inner walls tighten as I was lifting her up, I pulled my lips from hers and watched her face. I wanted to see her as she came, as I took her over like no other man had.

Bottoming back out in her womb, the orgasm hit her like a tidal wave. She tightened on my cock so much, so quick, that the tingle in my back was a mere thought as I emptied into her. I continued to move us at a slow pace, drawing it out for both of us. Her face was tilted back against the tile and her mouth was open on a long low wail that had me gripping her ass hard enough to leave bruises later. Her nails dug into my shoulders and flexed with each stroke.

Just because I didn't want it to end, I reached down with one hand to gently caress her clit. Her body clenched around me like a vice and the tingle in my back came back. That couldn't be possible. The muscles in my legs started to shake from the strain. Moving us so that I sat on the floor of the shower with her straddling me, never disconnecting our bodies, she started to ride me. Hard and fast. Slow and steady was gone; now, we chased a second set of orgasms that had us both crying out when they hit simultaneously.

"Holy shit," she gasped, panting in my ear where her head now rested on my shoulder.

"I was thinking 'holy fuck,' but that works too," I teased, running my hands up and down her back, holding her slightly against me so she didn't slide.

"Always have to have the last word," she muttered, nipping at my neck.

"Don't," I growled as my still semi-hard cock twitched inside her. "I don't think either of us is quite ready for another round just yet."

Another nip to the neck had me chuckling. This was the woman I knew hid under that tough professional exterior. When I thought my legs could hold me, I moved her so that I would take the brunt of her weight as we got up. My dick slid out of her and she moaned from the loss of contact.

"We aren't done yet, sweetheart," I whispered in her ear as I pulled her back under the now warm water. "I have to make up for lost time."

She shuddered against me, but slapped my belly lightly with a smile. We washed up silently, and I noticed that her body wash was beside mine in the stall and loved how they looked together. Sap. Yes, yes, I was when it came to her. Hopping out before she could, I grabbed my towel and wrapped it around my hips. Just as I pulled a second one off the shelf, she stepped out and I took her in before reaching out to dry her off myself. She did have a runner's body, but her hips and gorgeous chest were generous. They were perfect for a man to hold, squeeze, and grip. I bit my lip to hold back a groan and startled when her hands came up to cup my cheeks.

"I'm sorry," she said.

I knew what she was apologizing for and I wouldn't have it. Her reactions had been justified, given the situation. If I had been in her shoes, I would have done the same thing. I just had to figure out how to prove to her that they were just stories. I was hers, regardless of what they wrote, and I would never keep anything from her.

"Stop," I told her, putting a finger on her lips and leaning into her hands.

"I should have trusted you, Evan," she continued after moving back away from me a bit.

Dropping both towels, I quickly swept her up in my arms before hitting the light and carrying her to the bed. Getting us both situated under the sheets, I pulled her against me and she put her head on my pec while I ran a hand up and down her smooth back. Her fingers started to trace patterns on my chest and I sighed. I had missed the feeling of her touch, I had missed the way she totally relaxed when it was just us.

"We will get through this, boss lady," I said confidently.

"I know we will," she replied, a smile to her voice and something else I couldn't place.

Rolling her so I was looking down at her, I rested on my forearms so our noses touched. There was definitely a smile on her face; a large, happy one. It even had her eyes sparkling. Those three little words climbed my throat once again, but I swallowed them back down.

"Do you know something I don't know?" I asked, giving her an Eskimo kiss.

"For once, Mr. Foster, you will have to be the one in the dark."

JULIE

T HE PIECES WERE SLOWLY STARTING TO come together. It was like when you spent day after day, month after month, working on a puzzle and you got down to the those last few remaining pieces. Business was booming, Maggie had the last of the information on Ryan, and my lawyer had been updated and was pushing through with the divorce proceedings. I felt like a huge weight was being lifted off my shoulders.

Pulling up to Evan's house, I shut off the car and took it all in. It was complete. It still amazed me that it had all been done in such a short amount of time. Though, with Cooper and Evan working with the Grind crew, it shouldn't have surprised me at all. Those men were all driven and when family needed something, it got done.

The orange, yellow, and burgundy mums I had put on the

porch brought the feel of fall to the house, along with the changing leaves on the trees that surrounded it. Evan had opted for white wood siding to give the house the old farm feel and it had worked. The farmers porch that wrapped the house had two rocking chairs in the front, while the back opened up onto a small patio with a fire pit. It was perfect.

Letting out a sigh from the long day, I got out and made my way inside. The sun was setting and all I wanted to do was change and crawl into bed. I had worked late, ate at the office, and just wanted some sleep. The business would be closed for Thanksgiving Thursday and Friday, but I still had two more days to get through before that happened.

I didn't bother with the lights once I got in the door. Closing and locking it behind me, I beelined for the kitchen to make myself a cup of tea to take to the bedroom with me. As soon as the contractors had finished with the bedroom and we had moved the furniture in, I had started staying here. It hadn't even crossed my mind that Evan would care and I had quickly found out he hadn't at all. The memories of the night he had come home and I had surprised him in the shower still gave me chills.

While the water warmed, I turned and took in the interior. The living room, dining room, and kitchen had an open floor plan; he had wanted it that way for when there was company. He didn't want people feeling left out. How could you not love that about a man? Worrying about everyone else while he was building his own house. My heart thudded. Love.

I shook my head and concentrated on taking the rest in. The lights above the sink gave off a soft glow so I couldn't see much, but I knew that on the other side of the stairs was a hallway with a door to the master suite. It wasn't a huge room, but it was perfect for Evan and whoever he decided to make his wife. The thought of another woman living in this house made my stomach turn. Before I could dwell further, the chirp of the kettle let me know my water was boiling.

The smell of apple pie wafted up to my nose as I took my cup and made my way to the bedroom. I suddenly could hardly keep my eyes open. The days of working ten to twelve hours were starting to wear on me. I was looking forward to the holiday weekend. For once, I was going to take it off along with my staff. Avery wanted to put the final touches on the nursery, and I need to refuel for the coming stretch without her.

Placing my tea on the bedside table, I stripped down to my underwear and pulled on one of Evan's t-shirts that I had started wearing to bed. It still held the faint smell of him. I wasn't sure where we were headed, but for now I was going to enjoy the time I had him. When it was just us, I could be myself. I could drop the hard exterior I used in the office and just be a woman. His easy going nature and loving demeanor made it so simple. Huh. There it was again. Love.

Turning on the television, I found a romantic comedy and set the sleep timer. I knew I wouldn't last the entire thing and this way, it wouldn't end up on all night. I got under the covers and sipped from my mug. It wasn't long before my arms and eyelids were feeling like cement. Deciding not to fight it, I put the cup back on the table and snuggled under the covers.

What felt like minutes later, I was waking up to a room filling with sunlight. I had totally forgotten to set my alarm. Crap. Attempting to roll over, I found that the sun wasn't the only reason I had woken up. There was a weight over my side and a hairy leg tangled with mine, never mind the hard length pressing into my backside. When had he come home? How had I not woken up?

"Stop wiggling," his sleepy voice growled, his breath on my neck causing a shiver to run through my body.

I leaned into him and rolled my ass against his twitching cock. As exhausted as I still felt, a little morning loving would be a wonderful unexpected start to my day. Evan's arm gripped around me tighter, but that was it. Sliding my hand under the comforter, I reached around to him. I was going to stroke my hand down his side and around to his ass, but stilled when I realized he was completely naked under the covers.

"What's the matter, boss lady?" came the teasing question.

I wasn't able to utter a word because I was suddenly on my back with a gorgeous man between my legs, bracing himself up on his forearms. His weight on my body felt so good and had my lower body humming and pulsing in anticipation. It floored me how quickly I could be ready for him; I had never felt that with my ex. The smile helped, I concluded, looking into his baby blues and watching his lip twitch up so that his dimple showed.

"Surprise," he said, brushing my hair from my face.

"It's one I could definitely get used to," I told him, my hands coming up to run through his too-long hair.

"Me too," he whispered, leaning down to brush a kiss over my lips.

I closed my eyes with the sweetness behind it. Sighing, I opened them again when the contact was gone. Evan was watching me, and he looked like he wanted to say something. His eyes were darkened with lust, yet there was a hint of something else there. I raised my eyebrows in question. He shook his head, like he was clearing it, and when his eyes found mine again, the smile on his face was blinding.

The one on my own couldn't be contained. He did that to me. No matter how tired, moody, or pissed I was, he could always make me smile. I wrapped my legs around him and rolled my hips again, this time making sure to move my pelvis against his length. Pulsing from his cock had me moaning.

"That backfired didn't it, boss lady," he teased, pushing back against me. "Guess we will just have to take care of that."

"I can't," I replied, moving my legs and acting like I was going to push him off. "I have to get to work."

"Not gonna happen," he growled, leaning back down to trap me with his body and locking his lips on mine.

Knowing I wasn't really going to leave without this, I wrapped myself back around him. I dove my tongue into his mouth, yet stroked it against his slowly to change the pace. My legs latched on to his lower back to keep him close, but I didn't buck against him. I wanted to show him how I felt without saying it. I wasn't ready to say it.

He took the hint. His hand came down to run up my side and slip under my shirt. The skilled fingers he used on the guitar caressed my skin from hip to ribs, lazily making their way up to massage my breast. Nothing was hurried. His thumb ran over my peaked nipple, causing goosebumps to spring up all over my body. His free hand fisted in my hair, like he was afraid I would disappear. I locked one of mine into his as well and used the other to run along his arm over to his chiseled back.

I'm not sure how long we spent necking like a couple of kids, but eventually I felt my panties being tugged down. As Evan made his way down my body, planting open mouthed kisses as he went, I pulled off my shirt and continued to watch him. Once the fabric had been tossed aside and he had reached my toes, his eyes found mine and he crawled back up. Without the blankets in the way, I was able to take him in from head to toe.

His hair was mess from both travel and sleep, making my fingers itch to dive back into it. The muscles in his arms flexed, sending the tattoos dancing on both sides with each movement. I had noticed the new ink on his previously naked arm the last time we had been together. He said he had used it as a kind of therapy while he dealt with us being apart. His white ass was molded into two perfect globes and I couldn't wait to get my hands on them to pull him into me. When his eyes met mine, a sly smile curved his lips. Warm breath blew over my clit and my core clenched. I knew where he was headed, but there would be none of that today.

"I need you in me," I mewled.

The sound of my voice had him continuing his climb, the pace remaining slow and sensual. The smile widened as he got closer, the dimple showing deep in his cheek. I returned it and licked my lips for good measure, drawing his eyes down. Lust burned in them and the grin dipped a bit as his breathing quickened.

"What have I told you about playing with fire, Julie?" he asked, reaching for a breast with one hand and moving his mouth to hover over the nipple, never breaking our eye contact.

"Now," I pleaded, rising my hips to meet his.

Evan didn't hesitate as he found my center with his length and pushed inside, slowly, watching me as he did so. I closed my eyes for the briefest of moments as he sheathed himself to the hilt. When I opened them again, his were closed. When he started to rock slightly in and out, matching the beat with his suckling, he opened them again and looked at me. My hands didn't know where to go. I finally decided I wanted the best of both worlds; one went to his hair to hold him to my chest and the other to his ass to squeeze and keep him from pulling completely out.

Soon I felt the tingle of my orgasm climbing. My insides started to clench around his member and I felt him swell inside me. Still not changing his rhythm, he let go of my nipple with a *pop* and brought his mouth up. His tongue swirled around mine and slid against it. For the second time, the movements had me thinking about what it would be like to have his mouth on my clit. That was all it took. My wail of satisfaction was met with a long low growl as he filled me with his seed.

Tears sprang to my eyes as he collapsed on top of me, still connected at our most intimate parts. He must have felt them on his cheek as he nestled against my neck because he quickly shot up on his hands to look at me. I shook my head to let him know I was okay, but I couldn't get any words out because sobs soon started to escape me. I didn't even know what I was crying about. Evan got down on his forearms and wiped, along with kissing, away the trails being left, just causing me to cry harder.

"I didn't think I was that bad, boss lady," he teased, concern written all over his face.

"You weren't," I sniffed, slowly calming. "You were that good."

EVAN

"SO, YOU'RE ONLY HERE UNTIL Thanksgiving night?" Julie asked as we drove toward the office.

I hadn't been able to convince her to stay home in bed with me all day, but I had gotten another orgasm out of her while we had showered together. Now, I was driving her to the Maine office. I was still a little unnerved by her breakdown earlier because I couldn't shake the feeling it had to do with the magazines. Her cool, professional exterior was in place, yet the flush on her cheeks gave away the reason she had been late.

"Yeah, we have a concert Friday night in Florida," I told her. "We only have a couple more weeks and then we'll be home until June."

She nodded as I hit the blinker to turn into the parking lot. We had yet to discuss the long-term. I hoped she knew I wasn't going to let her go back to Massachusetts without a fight. I didn't want her to give up her business; however, I wanted her in my bed every night. Most preferably, for the rest of my life.

"I'll go grab us breakfast and be right back," I told her when I pulled to a stop, squeezing her hand before she could jump out of the truck.

"You don't need to do that," she returned softly, a small smile coming to her lips.

"I know," I admitted, "but I want to."

"No coffee though," she said, once she leaned in to kiss my cheek. "My stomach isn't liking it these days for some reason."

"How about a smoothie?" I questioned as she opened the door.

"That will work." She nodded, blowing me a kiss before shutting it and walking toward the building.

I was a little surprised by that action, so the goofy smile on my face was still there when I walked into the café down the street. The older lady behind the counter was sweet and knew that I was ordering for Julie, so she gave me exactly what she had been getting the past week or so. I heard whispers behind me while I was waiting for her to finish and found two college-age girls behind me sitting at a table. My guess was that they recognized me. Not wanting to create a scene, I moved my attention back to the woman putting two fruit smoothies and a paper bag in front of me.

"Thank you," I told her, grabbing the tray in one hand and the bag in the other.

Just as I was about to reach for the door handle, one of the women stood up and blocked my path. She was attractive enough, but I wanted to get back to my woman. Plastering my fan smile on, I stopped.

"Aren't you Evan Foster from Dark Roads?" she asked, one hand coming up to rest on my forearm.

"I am." I nodded, moving slightly so that her hand fell away.

"I'm so sorry to hear about everything going on with your ex-girlfriend," she apologized, a pout coming to her lips.

"My ex-girlfriend?" I asked, my smile wavering a little.

"Yeah." She gestured to a magazine on the table by her friend.

I shifted and noticed there was a picture on the front of Julie leaving her office in Massachusetts late in the day. She looked exhausted and she had a couple boxes in her hands, along with her work bag. The title read **Julie Lane loses business and Dark Roads' Foster**.

"Fuck," I muttered.

I put the bag of food on the travel tray and leaned down to grab the magazine, rolling it to stuff it in my back pocket. I was over this. Them going after me was bad enough, but they needed to stop harassing her. Clamping my teeth together, I pushed past the girl and grabbed the food again before I dropped everything.

"Do yourself a favor and don't believe everything you read," I hissed at her as I let the door go behind me.

I faintly heard her gasp, but I didn't care. Groupies were so gullible and ate up that shit like it was candy. It was a crap shoot whether it would help our sales or hurt them, yet I worried that it would do the latter for Julie's. I made the five-minute drive in two and jogged to the front door from my truck.

The receptionist at this office didn't know me, but she was on the phone when I walked in. Normally, I would have charmed her, but I was not in the mood and just walked past her. I figured it wouldn't be too hard to find Julie's office. When I heard my lady's soft giggles, I faltered a bit. She obviously hadn't seen the garbage in my pocket and I didn't want to ruin her day. I was just about to the door when I heard the responding laughter that sounded vaguely familiar.

"Hey, Ev!" Lexie greeted me as I stepped in the room.

"Hi," I stammered out as she tackled me in a bear hug.

Maggie followed suit, though she had flown Cooper and myself. The two had been sitting at the conference room table with Julie when I entered the room. All three had wide smiles and a small cake sat in the center of the table. As soon as our band's lawyer stepped out of my arms, I heard footsteps behind me.

"I'm sorry, Julie," she apologized. "I was on the phone when he came in."

"It's okay, Nicole," my girl assured her. "This is my boyfriend, Evan, and he can come and go as he pleases."

"Boyfriend?" everyone asked at once.

"Yes, boyfriend," she said, coming over to wrap one arm around my back, and rested her other hand on my abs.

The goofy smile came back and I leaned down to kiss her on the nose, causing her to giggle again and wrinkle it. God, I could hear that noise all day and never tire of it. Her hand found the magazine in my pocket and she tugged it out. My face fell.

"What this?" she asked, opening it.

"Some women had it at…" I trailed off because Maggie swiped it from her hands.

"That's the one I told you I couldn't stop because it was already printing when the paperwork went through," she informed Julie. "The retraction will be out in a few weeks."

"Gotcha," Julie said, grabbing the bag from my hand and digging in for her sandwich.

"What the hell just happened?" I questioned, my head bouncing between the three women in front of me as Nicole quietly excused herself and went back out front.

"What do you mean?" Lex asked as Julie took a huge bite of her breakfast.

"You knew about this?" I questioned my lawyer, gesturing to the article.

"Yeah…" she stuttered, looking from me to Julie and back again. "Julie didn't tell you?"

That had my girlfriend freezing mid-chew. She looked down at the sandwich in her hand for a moment. I watched her swallow and slowly turn to me. Her smile was meek and her eyes cautious.

"Evidently she didn't," Maggie concluded. "We found ties

between the parent company of the magazine, your mother, and Ryan."

"We?" I asked, my jaw clenching at having been left out of the loop.

"Lexie, Julie, and myself," she responded, moving to rest her hand on Julie's shoulder.

Lexie stepped over as well. Did I look like I was going to hurt her? Rolling my shoulders and releasing my hands, I realized I probably did. I had tensed from head to toe at the thought of my mother being involved in any of this, or having anything to do with Julie. I was supposed to be the protector. Taking a deep breath, I turned around and faced the door.

I didn't like that I had been left out of this, and I wasn't sure why or how Julie had been working with Maggie. I felt a hand touch my lower back and knew immediately by the feel it wasn't Julie. When another hand touched my arm, I looked over and found Lexie gazing up at me with soft eyes.

"Don't be mad at her," she pleaded. "She wanted to help take care of this since part of the problem was Ryan. She felt responsible for that."

"I'm not mad," I relented, my shoulders coming down a couple notches. "I just don't like being left out when this is something that affects me too."

Turning back around, I made my way to the conference table in a couple strides. Julie was sitting stock-still, her sandwich in her hand, and tears in her eyes. I got down on one knee in front of her, and my heart broke with the look on her face. I could see a million emotions racing across it, and I didn't like any of them.

"I'm not mad," I repeated, putting my hand on her thigh. "I just wish you would have filled me in."

"It all started when you and I weren't talking," she explained, her voice so quiet I almost couldn't hear it. "When things started to fall into place, it happened so quick that I didn't get a chance to tell you."

"Promise me one thing, boss lady," I requested, reaching up to wipe the few tears that had spilled free. "In the future, you let me know what's going on."

She nodded profusely, putting her sandwich down and cupping my face in her hands. I immediately stretched up to meet her lips in a kiss filled with love. Yep, it was time to tell her. I couldn't wait any longer.

"I love you, Julie," I whispered when I pulled back enough to rest our foreheads together.

"I love you too," she responded on a hiccup.

"On that note"—Maggie chuckled—"I have one more thing for you guys."

I stood up and turned to her, Julie's hands sliding to my chest as she moved with me. In Maggie's hand was an envelope. My eyebrows raised in question and she handed it to me with a smile. When I showed Julie, she motioned for me to open it.

My hands shook slightly since I wasn't sure exactly what the piece of paper inside was going to say. Would it be something to do with Ryan or my mother? Julie's hand now rested on my forearm and she squeezed it reassuringly. It was just what I needed to rip the flap open and reach in to pull out the small stack of papers. Seeing what was written at the top had my heart pounding in my chest and a sigh escaping my lips.

"About fucking time!"

JULIE

WITH THANKSGIVING BEHIND US, I had known that things would get a little crazy leading up to the birth of Avery's baby, but I hadn't anticipated just how crazy. The ten to twelve-hour days turned into fourteen and sixteen-hour days. I didn't even get a chance to bask in the fact that I was in a relationship with a wonderful, handsome, funny man who loved me. Instead, I was working three days a week in Massachusetts and spending the rest of my time in Maine.

"You do realize I can still work, don't you?" Avery asked, pulling me from the stack of papers and the computer sitting in front of me.

"I know," I responded, rubbing my eyes, "but you aren't exactly comfortable sitting at a desk these days."

When I looked up, she was rubbing her belly and looking down at it with a small smile. Her eyes eventually met mine and I smiled back. As tired as I was, I couldn't have been happier for her. I loved this woman like a sister, and I would do anything that needed to be done to ensure she was content. Since Cooper wasn't around, I wanted to make sure she was taken care of.

Lexie had moved back to Maine for the time being to help me with both offices, and was also taking the days I wasn't in the state to be with Avery. The guys were finishing up their tour and from what I got when I did talk to Evan, Cooper was chomping at the bit to get home. I couldn't lie, I was just as antsy to have them here. Six months was a long time without them around full-time. The holidays had been great, but they definitely weren't enough.

"Okay, so Jacobs, Miller, Wainright, and Mason?" I questioned, looking back down at my computer screen.

"Yes," she replied, shuffling papers. "And don't forget about Liberty."

I nodded and made a correction to the list. We were in Avery's living room, with a fire roaring and surrounded by papers, our computers, and files. A small storm was dumping six inches of snow on the ground, so we decided to hunker down and do a last review of the clients that would need to be covered while Avery was on maternity leave.

I caught her rubbing her belly out of the corner of my eye before her hand moved to her back. Her face showed a grimace for a fraction of a second until she realized I was watching her. Shaking her head, she pulled herself up and made her way to the kitchen.

"Want some hot chocolate?" she asked as she waddled up to the counter and grabbed the kettle to fill it with water.

I nodded and rubbed my eyes again. It was already five o'clock and we had been at it since seven. Today was not a day I was going to get in twelve, never mind fourteen. My body was letting me know it was done. Saving the file I had been working on, I then closed everything down.

While I started to clean up, Avery continued to putter away in the kitchen. Suddenly I caught a whiff of something that had my stomach turning. I slapped my hand over my mouth and beelined for the upstairs bathroom, hoping like hell I made it. I had barely entered the room before I felt everything I had eaten for lunch coming back up. Not bothering to shut the door, I emptied the contents of my stomach.

After two separate power pukes, I flushed and sat down on the floor. Leaning over, I put my forehead against the cool side of the tub and sighed. When I heard quiet footsteps, I turned my head and found Avery leaning against the doorjamb with a smile on her face.

"What are you grinning about?" I mumbled, wiping my mouth on the washcloth she tossed me.

"Are you ready to take a pregnancy test now?" she asked with a giggle.

"A what?!" I sputtered, sitting up. "Why the hell would I do that?"

"Let's see," she started, tapping her chin as though she was thinking hard. "You've been tired, coffee turns your stomach now, and chips have become your go-to."

"Oh, God," I gasped, covering my mouth again.

My brain started to run in circles. Shit! We never used condoms at all the last two times he had been home because we'd never had to in the past. I couldn't remember the last time I had taken my pill. I hadn't thought much of it with the increase in hours. It couldn't have happened that fast, could it?

"You and Evan would make great parents," Avery told me, coming over and sitting on the side of the tub.

"We aren't anywhere near that in our relationship…" I started to say quietly before she put her fingers to my lips to silence me.

"Evan is about ten steps ahead of you." She chuckled. "He will be over the moon."

She was right about that much. Evan was definitely ahead of me in our relationship. I couldn't help but compare him to Ryan when my defenses were down, yet he was nothing like him. Evan was ready to make me his for the rest of our lives, in every sense of the word. I was just a little gun-shy still.

"Let's not get ahead of ourselves," I chided, getting up slowly to make sure I didn't upset my stomach that now seemed to be calming.

Avery got up, the smile still on her lips. She motioned for me to follow her and she left the room. I could hear her heading down the stairs, so I grabbed the washcloth to wipe it over my face. Making quick work of some mouthwash, I made my way back downstairs behind her.

My friend met me at the bottom and handed me two sticks. I took them and felt the color drain from my face when I looked at them. Was I really ready for this? Could I be a mom? Avery, taking my other hand in hers, broke me from my thoughts.

"One step at a time," she said, gesturing for the bathroom. "While morning is the best time to do this, let's find out now."

I followed her into her and Cooper's bedroom, into their master bath. She shut the door behind us—not like anyone was actually going to interrupt anyway, but did it more out of habit. Taking her lead, I went to the toilet and did my thing while she leaned against the vanity and again rubbed at her lower back.

"Are you okay?" I asked once I had put the test on the counter and moved to wash my hands.

"Just a little lower back pain." She waved me off. "No biggie."

"How long has this been going on?"

"Eh, just a couple hours. Too much sitting."

"Ummm, Ave, are you sure that's all it is?"

"I've had Braxton Hicks the last six months," she reminded me. "It's fine."

I wasn't convinced, but I wasn't going to harp on her. She set her phone and turned to me. Linking our hands together, I closed my eyes and took a couple deep breaths. Two minutes felt like an eternity when I opened them and the timer still hadn't gone off. Ave squeezed my hand in reassurance; as much as I appreciated her support, it didn't help. Then everything happened at once. The timer went off, I looked at the window on the stick, and Avery let out words that had me turning sharply to her.

"Uh oh."

"What?"

"We need to go," she replied quietly, her voice catching slightly. "My water just broke."

Sliding the stick into the pocket of my sweatshirt, I didn't question her. Avery changed her leggings and slid on a pair of boots that sat in her closet, while I grabbed her hospital bag and went to remotely start my car. We moved quickly and silently to make sure everything was off in the kitchen and we had what we needed for the short trip. While the weather wasn't the greatest outside, I had driven in worse, and we were only fifteen minutes from the hospital.

Once we were in the car, Avery called her doctor and let her know what was going on. Evidently her back pain had been contractions and had been going on longer than she had let on. I shot her a look as she continued to give details. When she got off the phone, she closed her eyes and started to breathe deep long breaths.

"How ya doing, sweetheart?" I questioned as I navigated down the snow-covered road.

"Okay," she answered, her voice stronger than it had been. "I just wish Coop was here."

"I know," I sympathized, reaching over with one hand to squeeze hers briefly before moving it back to the steering wheel. "We got this, though. I'll be right beside you."

Fifteen minutes turned into twenty-five with the condition of the roads, but Avery took it like a champ. I had gone to Lamaze classes with her, so we worked on her breathing and focusing. The frustration of knowing she couldn't reach her husband even if she tried was written all over her face. The guys were in the middle of one of their two final concerts and they wouldn't have their cells. We could call Lee, but she wasn't even sure if he was with the band.

I dropped her off at the door and once I saw she had made it inside, I parked as close as I could and all but ran back. Not knowing what the evening was going to bring, I shot a group text off to Evan, Cooper, Lexie, and Maggie, hoping that someone would be able to get in touch with the band and let them know what was going on. Her labor could go all night or it could last just a few hours; it was anyone's guess.

When I got to the reception desk, I found Ave sitting in a wheelchair with a nurse behind her. They were waiting for me and I saw her doctor making her way down the hall toward us. It was time. My friend's face showed a plethora of emotions, from pain, to sadness, to fear, and everything in between. Before we could be whisked away, I scooched down in front of her and took her hands in mine.

"We got this," I told her, leaning up to kiss her cheek and smiling reassuringly at her. "Let's go have a baby."

EVAN

"I CAN'T WAIT FOR THIS to be over," Cooper muttered under his breath as he moved past me.

We were sitting down in our dressing room, getting ready to eat a light dinner before our second to last show started. We were all getting antsy since we were nearing the end of our tour. I think everyone was ready for a break after a grueling six months on the road in what seemed like never-ending motion. I felt bad for Coop, especially knowing Avery was so close to her due date and we were a plane ride away.

"Is everything okay at home?" I asked, stuffing a bite of salad into my mouth.

"Yeah," he answered, moving his vegetables around on his plate. "They are getting a small storm, so her and Julie are staying home to finalize client lists for her maternity leave."

"But?"

"She just sounds off," he said, his voice getting quiet. "I can't put my finger on it."

"She's got Julie," I reminded him. "Boss lady will make sure nothing happens."

"I know." He sighed. "Thank God. That really does make me feel better. I just wish…"

"You wish you were there," I finished for him. "I get it. Who wouldn't want to be? Just remember, we're almost done."

He nodded, picking at his food and finally putting a bite into his mouth. His eyes looked unseeing across the room, and I reached over to squeeze his shoulder. I was worried about Avery as well—I think we all were—but knowing my girl was there with her made me feel better. Julie would take care of her.

I was also anxious for another reason, one that was literally burning a hole in my pocket. Reaching into my pants, I pulled the ring out and studied it. It was a two-carat solitaire diamond ring in white gold. As soon as I opened the packet with her divorce papers a few weeks ago, I had bought it. I wanted to make her mine in every way as soon as I could. The idea of it on her finger made my heart *thump* a little bit harder in my chest.

"Well, well, well," Maggie said, letting out a long whistle as she came over to sit down beside me.

"Do you think she'll like it?"

"She'll love it," she assured me. "It fits her."

"I hope so for the price of the damn thing," Matt scoffed from behind me as he peered at it over my shoulder.

"Leave him alone," Chris chided, causing us all to look back at him in surprise.

"What did you just say?" Cooper stammered.

Chris wasn't one to get after Matt for anything, especially something like this. The two of them seemed to be on the paths to lifelong bachelorhood. We were all taken back.

"After everything you two have been through," he continued, ignoring our surprised looks, "you deserve it."

"Speaking of which," Maggie said, shaking her head at Chris in disbelief. "It looks like everything has finally come full circle."

"What do you mean, Mags?" I asked, almost dropping the ring as I rushed to put it back in my pocket so I didn't lose it.

"Ryan is in jail and your mother is being charged as an accessory in his whole scheme," she filled us all in.

A collective *"Whoop!"* filled the room. I was stunned, too stunned to react. It was over, all over. The articles would stop. Julie and I could move on. The stress I had been carrying around finally felt like it had been lifted.

"What about a retraction?" I asked, thinking about the damage the magazine could have caused on so many levels.

"They will be printing it in their last issue," she said, smiling.

"Last issue?" Matt questioned.

"Yep, they will be closing shop," came Maggie's reply, with a fist punch.

"Fuck yeah!" Cooper exclaimed, pounding me on the back.

I grinned like a fool. Now I *did* have everything. I had my band, my girl, and my life back. While a small part of me was bothered that my mother was involved and would likely face jail time herself, it wasn't enough to damper my feelings of excitement. Looking around, my breath caught. The guys were hugging each other and Maggie. Everyone was grinning and celebrating.

Coop approached me and grabbed me in a bear hug, slapping my back. Wrapping my arms around him, I returned it. It felt so good to reconnect with my bandmates. With everything going on, it had felt like we were all going our separate ways. Now, we were stronger than ever and ready to finish up this tour with a bang.

"Okay, guys," Chris sounded above the noise. "Let's finish eating and go listen to the opening bands."

We all nodded in agreement and sat down to do as he suggested. That was something we had done up until this tour had started; we would always go out and listen to those priming the audience for us. It was a way not only to come together as a band, but to support those we traveled with. This time, it was a young married couple on their first tour, and a bright female bombshell that was as sassy as she was spunky.

Finishing up, we all checked our phones one last time before leaving them in the room. I saw Cooper's face fall when he found that he didn't have anything from Avery. Julie hadn't sent anything either, but I chalked it up to them being elbows deep in paperwork. Sending her a quick, *I love you <3* text, I slid my phone into my bag and followed the others from the room.

Maggie trailed behind us, answering her phone and waving us forward as she spoke with who sounded like her wife. Mikey and the other bodyguards surrounded us; there weren't many people in the halls, other than those that worked the venue, but groupies popping out of nowhere wasn't uncommon. I could feel goose bumps breaking out over my skin as we got closer and could hear the screaming of the crowd.

As much as I wanted to get back to Maine, this was what I loved to do. Performing was a drug like no other. It gave you a high that couldn't be described. I bounced on my toes as we slid out a door and made our way to the side of the stage under the cloak of darkness. From there, we could watch without the crowd knowing. We didn't want to take the attention away from those on stage.

Before we knew it, both acts were done and we were slipping back through the door. Behind the stage, we spent a couple minutes complimenting the acts on their performances before we moved to form a circle. We wrapped our arms around each other's shoulders and were quiet as Chris recited a quiet passage. One we each knew by heart and that he said prior to every performance we had ever done. We had written it as a band and used it to gear ourselves up, reminding ourselves how grateful we needed to be for what we got to do every day.

When he finished, we all hollered "Dark Roads" and got into

our zones. Cooper pulled the drumsticks from his pocket and moved them like he was playing a song in his head, Matt cracked his neck and his knuckles, Chris closed his eyes and took several deep breaths, while I bounced like a boxer and grinned like an idiot. Finally, after what felt like forever, the crowd grew quiet and the stage manager gave us the signal to head up. We each slapped Chris on the back on our way by—he would enter last, as he sang the opening verse for our new song, and found our ways to our instruments.

The beat from Cooper behind me had me tapping my foot and getting lost in the music. When the lights came fully on as Chris walked out, I let my fingers guide me through the song. My heart thumped along with the drums, and Matt and I grinned at each other over our lead singer's head. I'm not sure I would ever get sick of this. The traveling, sure, but the playing in front of thousands of people while they sang along to your songs. Nope, it would never get old.

I think it was our best show of the tour. Maggie seemed to think so too, as I could see her dancing around beside the stage with a few others who had won backstage passes. It wasn't until I caught her looking at her phone with a concerned look, all movement seizing, that I almost missed a note. She moved to make her way backstage, and I knew something was up, causing my stomach to drop.

We finished the last song and when the lights went out, we ran off the stage for a quick relief before the encore. Maggie was back there talking to Mikey, and both had looks I couldn't read. Nodding to him, she made her way over to me. My heart ricocheted to my throat. *Julie.*

"So, we have a slight problem," she said with a small smile.

"Oh?" I questioned, wiping at the sweat dripping down my face.

"Avery is in labor, and I'm not sure if I should tell Coop," she murmured for my ears only.

My brain went into overdrive. We had two songs left. If we

could at least get through this concert, we would only have to deal with bumping our last one. I also felt my heart calm a bit, knowing Julie was fine. A flight from here would take a few hours anyway.

"Don't," I said, causing her eyebrows to fly up. "Just get the bus and plane ready to get us out of here as soon as we get off the stage."

She looked like she wanted to argue, but knew that I wouldn't have said something that wasn't in Cooper's or the band's best interest. He could be pissed at me later. I didn't care. I knew he would rather make up one concert than two. We needed to finish the show.

It had never felt like two songs could be so long before. I was again smiling so much that my cheeks hurt and had to struggle to keep my focus enough that I didn't miss my cords. Excitement for Cooper and Avery coursed through me and the diamond on the ring would catch my leg every once in a while through my jeans, amping me up even more. All of our lives were about to change.

"Holy shit, was that awesome!" Matt hollered as we came off the stage.

"You're not fucking wrong, brother," Chris agreed, clapping him on the shoulder.

"It's about to get better," I told them, gesturing to where Maggie and Mikey stood with our bags.

"What's going on?" Cooper asked when Mikey handed him his, a smile wider than I had ever seen on the other man's face.

"We're heading to Maine, brother," his bodyguard informed him. "You're having a baby."

JULIE

"WELL, LITTLE LADY," I CROONED, "you are going to keep your father on his toes."

Rocking the bundle in my arms, I studied every little feature. Her blonde eyelashes resting on her smooth pink cheeks, her tiny fingers clenched in a fist, and her sweet lips curved into a pucker. She was perfect. I was already in love with her.

"You're a natural," Avery commented from behind me.

I turned and found my friend watching me with a tired smile. If I hadn't thought she was a champ before, watching her go through labor would have done it. Due to our timing at getting to the hospital, she had been too late to get an epidural. The woman had done it all medication-free, and I bowed down to her. She was amazing. The emotions had run extremely high when the baby had showed slight signs of distress and we had found out that Cooper wouldn't make it in time. However, she had grabbed on to my hand and we got through it.

Now, we were waiting for the band to get there. Avery had put her foot down about keeping all other members of the family out until Coop had the chance to see his daughter. Both sides of the family *and* her best friend were waiting impatiently in the waiting room to see them both. I was using the opportunity to snuggle and hold her.

"How did you not find out the gender?" I asked, mystified at the fact that until the doctor had pulled the baby out, Avery hadn't known what she was having.

"Coop wanted to be surprised." She giggled. "Well, he will be surprised all right. He was sure we were having a boy."

I laughed at the thought. Suddenly, the door was flung open, and I jumped nearly ten feet when it slammed against the wall. All four members of Dark Roads entered the room with Cooper in the lead. His eyes went to his wife first and then to me when he realized that I was holding his child. He froze and Evan collided with his back with an *umph*. His friend pushed him lightly, and he made the last few steps before stopping in front me.

"Here you go, Daddy," I whispered, placing his daughter in his arms. "Meet Emalee Marcia Hall."

His eyes immediately filled with tears as he looked down at her in his arms. Turning, he made his way to the hospital bed and sat beside his wife. I felt like we were interrupting a tender moment, but I couldn't pull my eyes away from them. Cooper brought his hand up to cup his wife's face and I saw him mouth *thank you* to her before he leaned down to brush a soft kiss across his newborn daughter's forehead.

I couldn't hold the tears back and felt them slide down my face. I almost came out of my skin when I felt arms slip around my waist and Evan's lips on my temple. I leaned into him, taking in his warmth and letting out a sigh. We watched the new family for a few moments before Evan moved his lips to my ear.

"You look pretty good with a baby in your arms," he whispered.

I smiled and moved our joined hands to my stomach. When I flattened them against it, he tensed behind me. For a fleeting second, I questioned his reaction, but it was gone as quickly as it had come when Avery's eyes met mine and she nodded slightly.

"How would you feel if it was ours?"

I barely had the question out when I was spun around and Evan's hands were cupping my face. Tilting my chin up, he looked into my eyes, searching. My lips curved slightly, my hands coming up to cover his.

"Are you? Are we?" he stammered.

"I'm pregnant," I told him quietly. "Cooper isn't going to be the only Dark Roads member with a crib on the tour bus."

The change in Evan's face was faster than any I had ever seen. His smile was the largest one yet, and his dimples were deep in his cheeks. Tears filled his eyes and quickly spilled over. I squeezed his hands and moved them to his waist to pull him to me. I'm not sure how long we held each other, both of us crying and smiling nonstop. When he pulled away, he put one hand under my chin and tipped it up for a kiss. One that took my breath away with the promises and love behind it.

Cheers erupted behind us when our lips parted. I couldn't have been happier than I was at that moment. I looked over my shoulder at our friends, and each one of them was smiling. Avery had tears streaming down her face as well.

"Oh, don't mind me, it's just the hormones," she said, and we all began to laugh.

When I turned back, my heart jumped into my throat as Evan was now down on one knee, a ring box in his hand.

EVAN

"Julie Elizabeth Lane, you stole my heart from our first night together. You've shown me what it's like to have someone love you unconditionally, and you've allowed me to return it. I want to spend the rest of my life showing you how much you mean to me, creating a family, and making you wonder what the hell you were thinking," he started, chuckles filling the room with that line. "I couldn't imagine my life without you. I love you more than I can put into words. Will you do me the honor of being my wife?"

I watched more tears flow down Julie's face, but her smile grew as she nodded slightly before she covered her mouth with one hand and held the other out to me. Sliding the ring on her finger, I stood and gathered her in my arms. It wasn't long before Cooper ripped her from them and swung her around, a giggle escaping her as her eyes met mine over his shoulder. I shook my head as I was pulled into a bear hug by Matt. Just as he let me go, I saw Avery beckoning me so I made my way to her while Chris took my woman from Cooper.

"I'm so happy for you two," she whispered in my ear as I leaned down to hug her. "You are exactly what she needs."

The words had tears filling my eyes all over again. I was just about to get Julie back in my arms when the doors burst open and Avery and Cooper's families filled the room, along with Maggie, Lexie, and Jen, Avery's best friend. Baby Emalee was handed around and Julie's ring was flashed. Congratulations, tears, and hugs continued.

After a while, I stepped back and just took it all in. Julie was currently being hugged and fussed over by Lexie while Maggie's hand went to her stomach. My lady's face was literally glowing. I had never seen her so relaxed and happy, and my heart was bursting with the knowledge that I had put it there. I was still trying to process the fact that I, too, was going to be a father.

"Let's say hi to your Uncle Ev," Cooper's voice broke into my thoughts.

I barely had time to register that he was setting my niece in my arms. Immediately, my eyes were drawn to her tiny face. Her eyes were open, but she was quiet and seemed to be taking everything in as well. She really was perfect, a wonderful combination of Avery and Cooper. I ran my finger down her soft cheek and leaned down to press a kiss to her downy head.

"I'll always be here for you, little one," I told her, touching her tiny hand. "When you don't dare call your father, you can call me."

"It goes both ways, brother," Cooper let me know, causing me to jump because I didn't realized he hadn't moved.

I looked up and nodded to him with a smile before turning my attention back to his daughter. She let out a large yawn and closed her eyes again as I started to rock her. It was hard to believe that soon I would be doing this with my own. Like Julie could sense I was thinking about her, I felt one of her small hands on my waist as the other came up to stroke Emalee's cheek.

"You look pretty good with a baby in your arms," she said, repeating my words back to me.

"Yeah?" I questioned, throwing her a smirk. "Sexy enough to take home and have your way with?"

"Maybe," she teased with a laugh.

I nudged Cooper from the conversation he was having with Dale and handed his daughter back to him. Turning, I wrapped my arms around my fiancée, pulling her flush against the growing hardness in my jeans. I was more than ready to take her home and celebrate, just the two of us.

"No maybe about it, boss lady," I growled with a chuckle. "You'll take me home and have your way with me."

"If you say so," she sassed back with a giggle.

This was the Julie I loved, the one usually only I got to see. I kissed her, lightly this time because I could easily get lost in her and forget we had an audience. Her nails dug into my forearms and when I stepped back, her eyes were almost black with desire. I took her hand in mine and started to tug her toward the door.

"See you all later," I threw over my shoulder as we went. "I'm taking my woman home to see if we can make twins!"

EVAN

The holidays always had me thinking about my childhood and how much my life had changed. This year was no different. As I sat in the living room of my now completed home and watched the fire, I couldn't contain the smile on my face.

Christmas the prior year had been a celebration. Cooper and Avery had welcomed their baby girl Emalee into the world, and Julie and I had found out we were going to be parents as well. I had also proposed, knowing I couldn't live my life without her by my side. What we hadn't known was that this year was going to truly test us.

Whispers from the monitor by the couch drew me from my musings. Julie was talking to our son, Caleb, and every time I heard it, my heart would warm and *thud* harder in my chest. I counted my lucky stars each and every day that I had the two of them. Her voice was soft and low as she talked to him, telling him he was a good boy and that he needed to go to sleep so Santa could come. He didn't know what she was saying, but I could hear his *coos* in return. Tears pricked my eyes.

Fifteen minutes later, after listening to her sing and rock him to sleep, Julie made her way down the hallway toward the living room. She had slipped into a candy apple red sheer baby doll dress before she came out and I almost choked on the sip of beer I had taken. Her curves were even more generous now that she had carried our child and my cock instantly grew hard in my pajama pants.

"You're going to give Santa a heart attack," I murmured as she sauntered towards me like a feline after her prey.

"Hmmm, maybe he will leave me extra presents," she whispered as she climbed up and straddled me on the couch.

"Fuck woman," I moaned as her cotton covered heat came down on my raging hard-on. "You know how to tease a guy."

"Who's teasing?" She asked with a sly smile as she rocked her hips and leaned down to nip along my neck.

"Wait? Were you cleared?"

"Yep, she called me today," Julie answered, reaching down to grab the hem of my tank top to pull it over my head.

While Julie had given birth back in July, things hadn't exactly gone as planned and we had been restricted from sexual activity until her doctor had given her the okay. Even though I was itching to be inside her, I was also concerned. I didn't want to hurt her.

"I'm fine," she assured me without my even voicing my concerns outloud. "I need to feel you in me."

I still had reservations, yet it was hard to argue when the woman was kissing and licking every inch of my neck and chest. I bucked my hips up when she bit gently on my nipple and clamped my hands down on hers to hold her against me. Julie purred in response and lifted her arms to pull her hair up on top of her head.

I bounced slightly and was rewarded with her gorgeous full breasts jiggling.

My control was being held by a thin thread. Using one hand to hold her by the back, I used the other to grip the bottom of her dress and pull it up and over her head. The minute the fabric was out of my way I latched onto a breast and suckled. Her hands came up to wrap around my head and hold it to her chest as she tilted her head back to let out a quiet moan. I wanted to hear her yell my name, but I knew we needed to keep the noise down to keep the baby sleeping.

Unable to wait any longer, I turned my attention to her other nipple while I used my hand to pull myself from my pants. When Julie felt what I was doing, she brought one hand down to pull her thong to one side. It was all the invitation I needed. Slowly, letting her set the pace, I slid into her. Once I was sheathed to the hilt her inner muscles clamped around me. At the same time I felt her teeth bite onto my shoulder to stifle her moan.

"You're so fucking tight," I growled low in her ear causing her to shudder.

"Evan, you feel so good," she breathed back.

I could feel the tingle in my spine and knew i wouldn't last much longer. It had been too long without her. Moving one hand from her ass, I brought it around to gently flick her clit. Her body started to convulse around my dick immediately and I pumped harder into her as I filled her with my seed.

Holding her tightly against me and rubbing her back as we both came down, I kissed the top of her head. The fact that we hadn't used protection came to my mind quick and hard, but I shook my head when I remembered we no longer needed it. Tears filled my eyes before I could stop them. Julie must have felt them as they spilled over because she quickly sat up, a look of concern on her face.

"What?" she asked softly.

Running my finger along the pink scar on her belly I shook my head. Knowing what I was thinking about, she closed her own eyes and let out a sigh. She had had her own time to deal with the hand we had been dealt, but I was still processing. Quietly, Julie got up, grabbed my tank top and pulled it on.

As she cleaned herself up, I gently tucked myself back inside my pajamas. When Julie returned she pushed me so I laid back on the couch, grabbed a blanket and covered us up. I rubbed my hands up and down her back as she traced my tattoos up and down my arms. My tears had since dried, but the emotions within me were still raw.

Julie's pregnancy had been perfect. Not one issue aside from the minor morning sickness. We had thought labor and delivery would be the same. Unfortunately it hadn't gone that way. Caleb had been breach with the cord around his neck. It had been stressful and unnerving to end up with an unplanned c-section, but my wife had taken it like a champ. When they pulled my son from her, it had only taken seconds before his cry had filled the room, and we both let out a sighs of relief. I still remembered it.

"Let's see what we have here," the doctor said as she put her hands into Julie's belly.

"Why couldn't we have found out what we were having?" I muttered to my wife as I absently caressed her head and watched the doctor anxiously.

"Because it's fun," Julie answered with a little giggle.

Despite the stress of knowing the baby was breech and that the cord was wrapped around its neck, both she and the doctor seemed relatively relaxed. I was the exact opposite—my knees danced under the hospital gown I wore and I couldn't stop moving my hands. When Julie smiled at me, I leaned down to place a kiss on her forehead.

"It's a boy!" the doctor called out.

I looked up and saw the doctor pulling him out and expertly removing the cord. Seconds later, a loud wail filled the room as a nurse took him to clean him up and check him over.

My boy. My son.

With a smile on my face and tears in my eyes, I leaned back down to kiss my wife. Only, something wasn't right. Her eyes had started to roll back in her head and loud, insistent beeping filled the room.

"Mr. Foster, you're going to have to step out," a nurse said, pulling on my arm.

"Wait! What's going on? Julie!" I pushed back against her arm to reach for my wife when the beeping got louder and sounded much like it did on those damn TV shows she watched.

"She's coding!" the doctor yelled, then looked over to see I was still standing there. "Dammit. Get him out of here!"

Before I knew what was happening, the room turned into complete chaos. Nurses and doctors scurried around like ants during a rainstorm, blood was everywhere, and machines were sounding like sirens. I couldn't breathe. My chest started to constrict and I was suddenly shoved from the room into the hallway.

"Julie," I whispered hoarsely as I fell to my knees, tears streaming down my face.

I couldn't lose her. She completed me, she made me whole. There was no way I could raise a baby on my own, no way I could survive without her. A sob escaped me and I buried my face in my hands. I didn't care who saw me or heard me. I let out everything in that hallway. My cries, my sobs, my prayers.

"I got you, buddy," I heard, as strong arms wrapped around me, bringing me against a solid chest.

"I can't lose her, Coop," I blubbered, tears still sliding down my face uncontrolled and sobs wracking my body.

"You won't," he promised, his voice laced with uncertainty, even with the strength behind it. "How's the baby?"

"It's a boy," I whispered when I could catch my breath. "His name is Caleb. Caleb Michael Foster."

"Strong name for a strong little boy, just like his father," he assured me as he helped me to my feet. "Let's go tell the others."

Cooper was my rock in that moment. My brother, my best friend. He pulled me to my feet and into the room with the others.

We waited, prayed, and waited some more. I swear I had ten years taken off my life that day.

Finally a nurse had come and taken us to my son, there was no word on Julie. Hours later, after everyone had *oohhed* and *aahhed* over Caleb, a doctor finally came out and delivered the news. In order to save my wife they had had to remove her uterus. There would be no more babies in our future unless we adopted. At that point all I had been worried about was the fact that she was alive.

After a few complications, she had finally been released from the hospital. She had spent another couple months on bed rest and unable to do anything without my help. I had been so wrapped up in caring for both her and Caleb that I still hadn't processed that we wouldn't be able to have any more of our own. Now, with her in my arms and my baby's breathing coming over the monitor, it was hitting me like a ton of bricks.

"I love you, boss lady," I whispered, kissing her head.

"I love you back," she murmured, as her breathing evened out and she fell asleep.

Despite the fact that we couldn't have any more children, I was happy with what we did have. Caleb was perfect and thriving. His little smile and baby blues melted my heart every time he turned them on me. And Julie, there were no words for how grateful I was that had able me keep her. She was my everything. My feelings for her grew every day and my admiration for her as a woman had grown with the birth of our son. I was one lucky son of a bitch.

As always, I have to start by thanking my husband. Justin, I know you hear this all the time, but I wouldn't be chasing this dream without you. I love you and appreciate all that you do for me more than you will ever know. Forever and always.

My book team, Eric Battershell, Ryan Harmon, MG Book-covers & Design, and T.E. Black Designs, you've all been amazing! I can't tell you enough how much I appreciate the work and time you've contributed to this book. I'm so lucky to have you all!

Jenn Wood, my friend, my editor, my cheerleader. Woman, I'm not sure you knew what you were getting into when we started, but I'm glad you didn't. 🙂 I love you and am blessed to have you working on my babies.

Nancy Holstead Johnson, without you, this book wouldn't have even been written. Thank you for planting the seed that led to Evan's book. I'll forever be grateful.

Katreana Youland, my person, my best friend. Girl, I don't know what I'd do without you beside me. You're always as excited as I am about every little step and I love you for that. Squirrels for life. <3

Jen Harris and Jessica Woodcock, you've been with me from the get-go. That alone means more than I could ever put into words. I love you both. Keep those texts coming!

Heather Lyn, my Maine girl, the one who understands my crazy and yet still loves me for it. I'm so excited for our mini-collaboration in this book. Can't wait to see what our book futures hold.

Melissa Pascoe, my PA, my newest team member. You've been a gem and I'm so lucky to have found you! (Thank you, Jenn Wood!!) I can't thank you enough for your help with everything thus far. Crossing my fingers I don't scare you off too soon. ☺

My readers, you are and continue to be the reason that I do this. The messages and love I've received keep pushing me when I feel like giving up. Thank you all for the love and support you've showered me with.

Marcie Shumway is a small-town girl, born and raised in Maine. She resides with her high school sweetheart on a family-owned farm just miles from where she grew up. Her hubby and their four furbabies are her first loves, but they are followed closely by her writing, apple pie, and chocolate.

Marcie started writing short stories in middle school for her classmates to enjoy. They were always love stories with happy endings and spurred her dream of being a published author. Chasing that dream as an adult, she continues to write stories for her readers to love. An avid reader herself, Marcie thrives on the books of her favorite authors and when not writing, can be found curled up in her favorite spot with a good book in hand.

Made in the USA
Middletown, DE
17 October 2022